MAFIA WARS

YOUNG IRISH REBELS PREQUEL

BY VI CARTER

O'REAGAN
AN CHLANN

I'm the villain in most people's stories.

Ruthless, wealthy—the O'Reagan name demands respect. No one would ever call me reckless. But when I discover my maid, Luna, bearing bruises left by her so-called boyfriend, I snap.

There's a fragile beauty to her innocence, and her vulnerability does something to me I can't ignore.

So I take matters—and the law—into my own hands.

In broad daylight, I walk right up to her boyfriend and pull the trigger, ending his life and starting a war I hadn't anticipated.

He was the son of a powerful gangster, a man who wants Luna back and vengeance for his son's death.

But he's getting neither.

LUNA IS MINE NOW. AND I'LL SCORCH THE EARTH TO KEEP HER.

WARNING

This book is a dark romance. This book contains scenes that may be triggering to some readers and should be read by those only 18 or older.

NEWSLETTER

Join my newsletter and never miss a new release or giveaway by scanning the QR code below:

CHAPTER ONE

O'REAGAN
AN CHLANN

Luna

I stare at the text message, my hands trembling as I clutch the edge of the counter to steady myself. The word *cleaner* seems to glare back at me. It's pathetic, really—four years of nursing school, endless shifts at the hospital, and this is what I'm reduced to. But then again, what choice do I have?

I rub my temples before throwing my head back and staring up at the ceiling. Mark was a charmer, a good guy when I met him; I honestly thought I had struck gold. That was until he slowly started changing. It was in small ways at first, him dictating who I hung out with, asking me to sit in with him instead of going out with my friends; I had just thought it was love. An infatuation that honestly made me feel special at the time. How stupid was I?

Behind me, I hear the heavy tread of footsteps, each one sending a spike of dread into my chest. I don't turn around. If I meet his eyes, it'll only make this harder.

"Why the hell are you just standing there staring at the

ceiling?" Mark growls. His voice grates against my nerves, low and sharp like the flick of a blade. "You make dinner yet?"

Dinner. Right. God forbid I forget *his* schedule.

"I—I was going to," I stammer, snatching my phone closed and shoving it into my pocket. My fingers brush the bruises on my hip, fresh from last night's outburst, and I swallow hard. "I just needed to grab some things first from the store."

"You better hurry the fuck up, I'm starving." He's close now, close enough that I can feel the heat of his body against my back. I freeze as his fingers trace the curve of my neck, deceptively soft, before they curl into my hair and tug just hard enough to sting. "You're lucky I put up with you, you know that?"

Lucky. That word burns as much as his grip. I nod stiffly, my eyes glued to the sink, counting the seconds until he lets go.

He finally releases me with a grunt and stalks toward the living room, muttering under his breath about how useless I am. The door slams shut behind him, and I let out a shaky breath; my fingers press against the edge of the counter to keep myself upright.

This can't be my life. It can't. I had escaped one hell hole and ended up in another. It's like bad luck followed me around. Only with Mark, it was a slow cruise down a crumbling road. With my parents, that was different.

My parents were city people—fast-talking, fast-moving, and fast-falling into the grip of whatever had them hyped up that day. The city lights might as well have been needles; the streets smelled of sweat and urine. I was a shadow in their world, a ghost who remained invisible until I wasn't.

I don't know what shifted. Maybe it was my body changing,

or maybe it was the weight of desperation in my father's slurred voice. One night, I heard them—whispering, plotting. A new way to score. But it wasn't drugs they were planning to sell. It was me.

"I'm telling you, she's ready," Dad's voice rasped, wet and raw, like he'd been screaming at the walls. "You just gotta ease her into it, y'know?"

I froze in the dark hallway, the thin carpet rough under my bare feet. My breath caught in my chest, hot and sharp. Ready? Ready for what? Then I heard the laugh—the low, knowing chuckle of his friend, a sound that made my skin crawl.

I didn't wait for the rest. I grabbed what little I had—a tattered hoodie, a few crumpled bills from the kitchen counter—and I ran. The air outside was biting, but it felt cleaner than anything in that house. My legs carried me faster than I thought they could, through the alleys, past the shouting drunks and flickering neon lights.

I thought I'd escaped. I thought I'd found freedom.

But freedom wasn't waiting for me at the end of that sprint. He was.

He found me huddled in the corner of a bus station, my hoodie pulled tight over my head, my knees drawn to my chest. His smile was warm, disarming, but his eyes... God, his eyes were empty.

"You look lost," he said, crouching in front of me. He smelled of something spicy—like cloves, maybe—and something else. Something cold and metallic, like a blade, kept too close to the skin.

I didn't know what he was then. How could I? I thought monsters were loud, angry, and obvious. But he was quiet. Careful. Patient.

3

And I ran straight into his arms.

I glance at the clock. He'll be gone in a few hours, off to whatever shady deal he has lined up tonight. It's the only time I get to breathe, and even then, the air feels thin, suffocating. I take the phone out of my pocket again and read the message from Becca one more time. A soft noise behind me has me freezing, and I glance over my shoulder, but no one is there. I push the phone back into my pocket, as deep as the fabric will allow.

It's not the kind of job I'd ever imagined for myself, but if it means I can get out—even for a few hours—I'll take it. My friend Becca swears it's safe, or at least as safe as it can be, when you're working for people like this. Mafia, she said. Big players. The kind of people Mark only wishes he could run with.

I've seen enough of his world to know what that means— money, power, danger. But Becca's been doing this job for months, and she swears they leave the staff alone. "They don't care about us," she told me. "As long as you do your job and keep your mouth shut, they won't even notice you."

I don't believe that entirely. People like that *always* notice. But it's my only way out. Mark will never let me work as a nurse again—he made that clear the day he slapped me for applying to the hospital without asking his permission. But a cleaning job? A maid? That's just low enough for him to approve.

The thought makes me sick, but I'll take it. I have to.

The fluorescent lights in the store buzz faintly. I grab a packet of steak and toss it into the basket, my fingers brushing against the cold plastic. The thought creeps back, uninvited, like it always does—poison. Just a fleeting notion, nothing more, but it lingers longer than I'd like.

"You're crazy," Becca's voice echoes in my head. *"Just leave him."*

Easy for her to say. Becca doesn't have to answer to Mark. She doesn't have to figure out how to survive with no job, no money, and no family. The day I left was the last day I saw my parents; no one rang the Gardai and reported me as a missing person. That shouldn't have hurt, but even the thought of it still stings deeply.

"You can live with me." The conversation with Becca keeps circling around in my mind as I walk around the supermarket. Her flat is already bursting with two roommates, barely enough space for her, let alone me.

But this job…this job could be my chance. If I can hold onto it, save every penny, I could escape. My steps feel lighter at the thought, my chest loosening as I toss a bag of garlic-spiced potatoes and some fresh vegetables into the basket.

I spot her in the next aisle over, a young mother with a boy who can't be more than four or five. She's crouched beside him, holding up a box of cereal while he chatters excitedly. It's not what she's saying, or even what he's saying; it's the way she looks at him—like he's her whole world. Like nothing else in the store, in the city, in the universe matters except that little boy's smile.

Pain stabs through my chest, sharp and relentless. I press my hand against my ribs, but it doesn't help. It never does. I try to look away, to focus on the cans of soup I don't even need, but the sight of them stays burned into my mind. The boy's bright eyes. The mother's soft laugh.

I tell myself to move, but my feet stay rooted. That kind of love, that safety—it feels like something from a dream I've forgotten how to have. My throat tightens. I try to swallow, but it's like the lump in my throat is made of razor blades.

I've gotten good at burying my past. Shoving it down, locking it up, and pretending it's not there. But today, it feels like someone struck a match and set fire to every lock I ever forged. It's all right there, raging and hungry, refusing to be ignored.

I shouldn't have stayed out with Becca last night. I shouldn't have dared to steal a moment for myself, shouldn't have laughed too long or drunk too much or forgotten, even for a second, what was waiting for me when I got home. But I just wanted one night—one night where I wasn't watching the clock, wasn't bracing for the storm.

One night to be me. To remember who that even is.

The boy giggles, tugging at his mother's hand as she places the cereal in the cart. She leans down, brushing his cheek with her knuckles, her face glowing with love.

I feel hollow, as if something essential has been scraped out of me, leaving nothing but a shell that somehow still aches. I tighten my grip on the basket and force myself to turn away.

Love like that doesn't live in my world. It never has.

When I get home, the familiar weight of dread sinks into me, but I shove it down. I cook the meal with care—steak perfectly seared, potatoes golden and fragrant, vegetables steamed just right. The aroma almost makes me smile. Almost.

Mark's lounging on the couch when I bring his plate to him. The TV blares some mindless show, but his eyes land on me with that sharp, dissecting look that always seems to cut me open. My stomach churns.

"Why the nice dinner?" he asks, his voice thick with suspicion.

I force a smile, but it feels brittle, like it might shatter at any moment. "I got a job," I say, hating the way my voice shakes. Weak. Always so goddamn weak.

Mark tilts his head, his fork pauses mid-air. There's a warning in his narrowed eyes, a challenge I've seen too many times. "A job?"

"A cleaner," I blurt out quickly before he can twist the question into something more dangerous.

He scoffs, the corner of his mouth twitching up in that cruel grin. "Cleaning piss pots?" He lets out a low chuckle, stabbing a piece of steak and shoving it into his mouth.

I swallow hard and nod, keeping my head down. "It suits you," he says, turning the volume up on the TV.

I stand there for a moment, the tray still in my hands, my jaw clenched so tight I'm afraid my teeth might crack. A small voice inside me, the one that still fights to exist, whispers: *One day, I'll be gone. One day, you'll choke on that grin.*

I turn to walk away, but his hand springs out, his fingers tightening on my wrists; the pain is instant, but I've learned not to flinch. "As long as my dinner is on the table, you can take your pathetic job."

I should thank him; he hasn't released my wrist; I know he's waiting for my gratitude.

"Thank you," I whisper, and he releases my wrists turning back to his TV.

But for now, I retreat to the kitchen, where the knife I used to cut his steak still glints on the counter. The thought brushes past again, tempting. This time, it lingers.

Mafia Wars

CHAPTER TWO

O'REAGAN
AN CHLANN

Luna

The next morning, I stand outside the iron gates of the estate, my stomach churning as I clutch my purse to my side and watch the taxi sail away. That's ten euros I'll have to give back to Mark straight away, but it's the best ten euros I've ever spent. The house in front of me is massive, a sprawling mansion surrounded by tall, manicured hedges and cameras that swivel lazily as they track my movements. I feel the weight of them as I press the intercom, my heart pounding against my ribs.

"Name?" a man's voice crackles through the speaker.

"Luna," I say, my voice trembling. "Luna Tobin. I'm here for the cleaning job."

There's a pause, then a loud buzz as the gates swing open. I step through, my sneakers crunching against the gravel driveway as I make my way toward the house. The front door is twice my height, dark wood with an intricate brass knocker shaped like a lion's head. Before I can knock, it swings open.

A woman in her forties stands on the other side, her dark hair pulled back into a tight bun. Her eyes scan me from head to toe, taking in my cheap, secondhand clothes and scuffed shoes.

"You're late," she says curtly, stepping aside to let me in.

"I—I'm sorry," I stammer, but she's already walking away, her heels clicking against the marble floor.

The foyer is even more overwhelming than the outside—high ceilings, crystal chandeliers, and a sweeping staircase that looks like something out of a movie. I feel like I've stepped into another world, one where I don't belong.

"This way," the woman says, leading me down a long hallway lined with dark wood paneling and expensive-looking artwork. "You'll start on the ground floor; the library and the main living room need a deep clean. All supplies are in the supply cupboard, three doors down to your left. Stay out of the main office and the basement. And whatever you hear, whatever you see—" She stops and turns to face me, her eyes narrowing. "You didn't."

I nod quickly, my palms sweating.

"Good," she says, handing me a set of keys. "These are for the supply cabinet; if anything goes missing, I know who to blame." My fingers curl around the keys, but I have this overwhelming urge to throw them back. "Don't make me regret this."

I head to the cupboard, my footsteps echoing faintly in the empty hallway. Pulling open the door, I grab the cleaning supplies—a caddy filled with sprays, cloths, and a new feather duster. With everything in hand, I make my way back to the library.

The moment I step inside, I freeze. The sight before me steals my breath. Rows upon rows of books stretch endlessly, their

12

spines gleaming under the golden light streaming through the high windows. Dust dances in the air like tiny stars, and for a moment, all I can do is stand there, staring in awe. A noise down the hall has me quickly closing my mouth and getting to work.

As I start my first task—dusting the shelves in one of the guest rooms—I can't help but feel like I'm being watched. The house is too quiet, the kind of silence that makes your ears strain for the faintest sound. I try to focus on the work, scrubbing at a stubborn stain on the window, but my mind drifts.

This is better, I tell myself. Better than being at home, waiting for Mark to come back. Better than tiptoeing around him, trying not to set him off.

But as I hear the low murmur of voices down the hall—deep, commanding tones that send a shiver down my spine— I fear I might have made a mistake.

One of them cuts through the rest—a voice so strong and deep it practically rolls across my skin. It's the kind of voice that could send shivers down your spine, equal parts intimidating and mesmerizing. I'm not sure which it's doing to me right now.

Before I realize it, I'm moving toward the door, drawn in by the rumble of his tone. I stop just shy of the threshold, listening, my pulse quickening as the voice grows closer. Then, it stops, and the sound of heavy footsteps fills the hallway. My heart leaps as the footsteps slow, and a massive figure passes the doorway.

I duck my head, instinctively trying to make myself smaller, but it's futile. The man pauses, and to my disbelief, he steps back, filling the doorway entirely. I look up—then up again. He's a giant, towering close to seven feet tall. His dark brown eyes lock onto mine, so deep they're nearly black, and for a moment, I forget to breathe.

"Who are you?" His dark eyes narrow, suspicion darkening his already intimidating features.

"Luna." My voice comes out so high-pitched it practically squeaks. Mortified, I wave the duster like a ridiculous little flag. "The new cleaner." Oh God, I sound so dumb.

He doesn't say a word at first, just lets his gaze rake over me, from the messy bun on my head to my scruffy shoes. My skin prickles under his scrutiny.

"Have you been eavesdropping?" His voice drops an octave, and my stomach twists. I pale, shaking my head so fast it's a wonder I don't give myself whiplash.

"No! Of course not!" I stammer, my pulse hammering like a drum.

He takes a step toward me, closing the distance, and I swear the air in the room gets thinner. "It seems like you were snooping."

I swallow hard. "It's my first day," I manage weakly, hoping the words will buy me some slack.

He laughs, but it's not a laugh filled with warmth or humor. No, it's the kind of laugh that could chill you to the bone, a sound born of a man who's long forgotten what happiness even feels like. "Let's not make it your last," he says, smirking as he turns to leave; he winks before disappearing, leaving me frozen in place until my lungs finally remember how to work. I suck in a shaky breath.

It's only my first day, and I'm already counting down the three shifts I have this week, praying they'll fly by. But the second

14

I leave, something strange happens—I start looking forward to coming back. That's not normal. Not for me. And definitely not after an encounter like that.

He haunts my thoughts, his giant frame and those dark, all-seeing eyes intruding on my dreams. What's wrong with me? How can I find someone like that—someone who radiates danger and violence—so...magnetic? It's like I'm a magnet for the worst kinds of people.

The next three shifts pass in a blur, though not without a few heart-pounding moments. I learn his name from the other cleaner, Sara. Cian. A name as sharp and dangerous as the man himself. And when she confirms what I'd already suspected—that he's mafia—it should be my cue to steer clear. To stop lingering in the hallways, ears straining for the sound of his voice. To stop hoping for a fleeting glimpse of him.

But I can't. I can't stop. Every time I hear his deep, commanding voice in the distance, my pulse spikes. Every shadow that moves has me glancing up, half-hoping, half-dreading that it's him.

This is bad. So, so bad. And yet, I'm helpless to stop it.

There is definitely something wrong with me.

I finished my shift, and I'm exhausted today. I think it's more mental than physical. I push the keys into the front door, and my stomach tightens as I step inside. The smell of whiskey hits me first, sharp and sour, and I know before I even see him that it's going to be one of those nights. Mark is slumped on the couch, a bottle dangling from his fingers, his eyes fixed on me like I'm prey.

"You left the damn freezer door open," he slurs, his voice low but charged, like a thunderstorm about to break.

"What?" I blink, confusion flashing through me. "I wasn't even—"

"Don't lie to me!" His shout cracks through the room, and I flinch. "You let everything thaw out. All that food, wasted. You think I don't know you did it on purpose?"

My pulse races, a thud-thud-thud that I feel in my throat, in my ears. "I didn't," I say, my voice trembling. "I wasn't even near the—"

"Shut up!" The bottle slams onto the coffee table, whiskey sloshing over the edge. He stands, his movements jerky and unsteady, but that doesn't make him any less dangerous. His eyes are wild, dark, with something that makes my skin crawl.

"I didn't do it, Mark," I whisper, backing toward the kitchen. "You have to believe me."

"Believe you?" He laughs, a cold, humorless sound that freezes me in place. "You think I'm stupid? You think you can make a fool out of me?"

"No, I—"

"Don't lie!" His voice roars, and suddenly, he's moving, closing the distance between us. I can't breathe, can't think. My back hits the counter, the edge biting into my spine, and I'm trapped.

His face is too close, his breath reeking of alcohol. "You're lying," he says, quieter now, but somehow that's worse. His eyes burn into mine, and I can feel the rage radiating off him like heat. "And you'll pay for it."

Tears blur my vision, but I can't let them fall. Not now. Not in front of him. I press my palms against the counter, trying to ground myself, trying to keep from shaking. But my heart is racing, my mind screaming at me to do something, anything, before this gets worse.

And I know it will. It always does.

CHAPTER THREE

O'REAGAN
AN CHLANN

Cian

The water is scalding, just how I like it, pounding against my shoulders as I lean one hand against the shower wall. Steam fills the bathroom, curling into the corners like smoke, but it does nothing to clear my head. Nothing does.

I close my eyes, tilting my head back under the spray, letting the hot water pound against the tension coiled in my neck. The day's been long—too long—and my patience is a thread stretched to snapping. Another blowout with Uncle Finn over shipment routes. Same old argument, different day. His way or mine. Except his way always leaves loose ends—and loose ends are dangerous. Then there was Jason, the screw-up of the century, botching the drop-off. Why the hell we still let that idiot near the business is beyond me. The whole thing's a mess, and, as usual, it's fallen to me to clean it up.

The water doesn't wash away the weight pressing down on

my shoulders, and the ache at the base of my skull only grows sharper. My mind spins, replaying every misstep, every bad call, until my teeth grind together. I hate mistakes. Hate inefficiency. But most of all, I hate the sense that things are slipping through my fingers like water down this drain.

I let out a frustrated breath, my hand drifting lower as I try to find some kind of release, something to take the edge off. The image comes unbidden—one of the dancers from the club last night, dark-eyed and curvy, her dress clinging to every inch of her body. I'd thought about taking her home, but the idea of answering her the next morning killed the mood. I don't do strings, and women always seem to want them, and I wasn't a guy who used the back rooms in the club; I didn't like using someone else's bed.

The water slides over my chest, and I wrap my hand around myself, letting my mind wander. For a moment, I'm somewhere else, not in this house, not in this life. Somewhere quieter, freer. It's just me and the dancer; she lowers herself to her knees and unzips my trousers. I stroke my cock as I envision her mouth warm and wet around it; she pushes my cock into the back of her throat; I let out a groan as I stroke harder, pushing deeper into her mouth, searching for the release. I pump harder, my hands wrapping around her long blonde hair, tightening against her scalp as I force her mouth up and down my shaft, moving her faster and harder. "Oh fuck, yeah!" I mumble, gripping my hand against the wall to keep my balance as I move even faster, rising on the tips of my toes to reach that place that will give me some freedom.

The illusion is smashed as a noise from behind me has my eyes snapping open, instincts kicking in like a live wire. I spin around, every muscle coiled tight, my hand flying to the gun concealed beneath the washcloth. The weight of it is a cold, familiar comfort—I even sleep with one under my pillow. My fingers curl around the handgrip, but I don't pull it out. Not yet. My gaze locks onto the shadow in the doorway, my fingers loosen their hold on the gun, and I withdraw my hand, leaving it in its hiding place.

It's her—the new maid. What's-her-name. Luna.

She freezes, her wide hazel eyes locked on mine, her mouth falling open as her gaze drops— to my engorged cock.

"Jesus Christ!" she yelps, spinning around so fast she nearly trips over herself. "I'm so sorry! I didn't—no one told me—"

I don't move. For a second, I just stare at her, my mind trying to catch up to what's happening. She's got one hand clamped over her eyes like that's going to erase what she just saw, and the other is fumbling with the door handle.

I should be pissed. Hell, I probably will be in a minute. But right now? I can't help it. I smirk.

"You got an eyeful there, sweetheart?" I ask, my voice low and teasing.

She makes a strangled sound, halfway between a gasp and a squeak, but doesn't answer.

"Turn around," I say, leaning against the wall of the shower, the water still beating down on my back. "You've already seen me naked. Fair's fair, don't you think?"

"No," she says immediately, her voice shaking. "I'm—I shouldn't be here. I'll just—"

I cut her off with a sharp laugh. "Oh, you're here, all right. And you're not leaving until we even the score."

21

"Even the—" She stops, her shoulders stiffening as she realizes what I'm saying. She shakes her head, her voice rising. "No. No way. This is insane. I—"

"Luna," I say, my tone softening, though there's still an edge of command in it. "Relax. I'm not going to hurt you. Just—turn around."

She hesitates, her fingers tightening on the edge of the door. I can see the tension in her shoulders, the way she's trembling just slightly. She's scared.

I like that.

But I don't push her. Not yet.

Finally, slowly, she turns. Her head stays down, her dark hair falling into her face, but I can see the flush spreading across her cheeks, her neck. She's wearing those baggy clothes again, the ones that make her look like she's trying to disappear. They don't do her any favors, but even so, there's something about her—something soft, vulnerable.

"Take them off," I say, my voice quiet but firm.

Her head snaps up, her eyes wide. "What?"

"You heard me." I tilt my head, watching her. "Shirt first."

She hesitates, her hands hovering near her arms as if she's debating whether to follow my command. The defiance in her eyes sparks something in me, but I keep my face impassive.

"Do it," I say, my voice low, but there's an edge to it that I know she can feel. It's not a request.

She stares at me like I've lost my mind. For a second, I think she's going to bolt. But then, slowly, she reaches for the hem of her

22

shirt. Her hands are shaking as she pulls it over her head, revealing smooth, pale skin and a thin tank top underneath.

"Keep going," I say, my eyes never leaving hers.

She swallows hard, her gaze darting around the room like she's looking for an escape. There isn't one. Finally, she slides the tank top off her shoulders, letting it fall to the floor. She isn't wearing a bra, and her breasts fall free, round and soft looking. My cock twitches, and her gaze travels down before she quickly glances away, but not before she sees my erection. Her hands immediately move to cover herself, but it's too late.

I take her in, my gaze sweeping over her. She's slimmer than her baggy clothes made me believe, but there's a quiet strength in her posture, a stubbornness in the way she holds herself.

"Turn around," I say.

"No." Her voice is firm this time, and for the first time, she meets my eyes directly. There's fear there, yes, but also something else. Defiance.

I smile. I can't help it.

"No?" I say while cutting off the spray of water and stepping out of the shower naked. I'm slow to grab a towel, letting her gaze linger on my body; even as she seems to fight with herself to look somewhere else, she can't seem to stop. "But you should know—I always get my way in the end." I wrap the towel around my waist.

She doesn't say anything. Instead, she slowly turns around. At first, I think she is obeying me, but instead, she gathers her clothes as quickly as she can. Her hands are shaking again, but she doesn't stop, doesn't look at me.

My jaw tightens as my gaze roams over the bruising on her

back, faint but unmistakable. Some are old, faded to dark shades; others are fresher, still red and blue.

I clench my fists at my sides. *Who did this to her?*

"How long?" I ask, my voice barely above a whisper.

She stiffens, but she doesn't turn back around. "How long what?"

"You know what I mean," I snap, my patience slipping. "How long has someone been using you as their personal punching bag?"

She whirls to face me, her eyes blazing with a fury that catches me off guard. "You don't get to ask me that," she spits, her voice shaking. "You don't get to stand there and question me about my personal life."

The words surprise me; no, it's not the words; it's the venom behind them. I step closer, closing the space between us. She doesn't back away this time, though her hands are trembling.

Her defiance falters, replaced by something I can't quite place—fear, maybe, or exhaustion. She drops her gaze, her arms wrapping around herself like she's trying to hold herself together.

"Who did this?" I ask.

"It's not your concern," she mutters so quietly I almost don't catch it.

"Yes, it is," I reply, my voice softening despite myself. "You're in my world now. And in my world, no one touches what's mine."

Her head snaps up, her eyes wide with shock.

"I'm not yours…" Her lips tremble, brows pulled down in confusion.

24

I've seen enough of her body to know she could be mine, in my bed for a few hours.

I smirk at her. "Oh, sweetheart. But, you are."

She quickly pulls her tank top back on and then her jumper, her cheeks blazing.

Once she fixes her top, she folds her arms across her chest. "Can I leave?"

"No." I tilt my head. The bruises need answering, too. A man hitting a woman isn't something I could tolerate. I want to know who the coward is.

"Who marked you?" I find myself saying, while glancing at her chest which is now covered, hidden under the baggy sweater. My cock jumped just thinking about how full her breasts were. How nice it would be to play with them.

"My boyfriend." She juts out her chin, a look of anger flashing in her deep hazel gaze.

I nod. "You can leave now."

She drops her arms to her side and quickly ducks out of the bathroom.

I'll have to find out more about her boyfriend, who thinks it's okay to hit her. I wonder how he'll feel when I unleash my wrath on him.

Vi Carter

CHAPTER FOUR

O'REAGAN
AN CHLANN

Cian

I drag the towel over my skin, the fabric doing little to match the storm brewing in my head. The decision is made. Luna's boyfriend needs to be dealt with—one way or another. I shove on a clean shirt, tugging it into place as I head out. No hesitation. No second-guessing.

It doesn't take long to find her. She's in the staff quarters, standing by the sink. A mug is in her hand, but she isn't drinking from it. No, she's just holding it, her movements slow and mechanical as she wipes the same spot over and over again. Her eyes are fixed on the red tiles in front of her, glazed and distant. What's going through her head right now? Guilt? Fear? Both?

Sara—one of the other staff, I think—sits at the corner table, her head bent over her phone. The moment she catches sight of me standing in the doorway, she jolts upright, her chair scraping against the floor. The sound pulls my focus briefly, but I wave it off. She's not who I came for.

"Hello, Mr. O'Reagan," Sara stammers, her voice stiff with forced politeness.

Her words slice through the room, and Luna jerks like a string has been yanked. The mug wobbles in her grip, and for a split second, I think she's going to drop it. Her face goes pale as death, and her eyes lock onto mine. Wide. Unreadable. But unmistakably afraid.

I step further inside, ignoring the rising tension that hums in the air like a live wire. "Come with me," I say, my tone flat and final.

Silence. A thick, suffocating kind of silence. Sara's gaze darts to Luna, and I can practically see the assumptions churning in her head. Luna, though, doesn't move. She doesn't speak. Her fingers tighten around the mug like it's her last lifeline.

"Now," I add, sharper this time.

That does it. Luna sets the mug down with trembling hands and follows me, her steps slow and reluctant. She thinks she's in trouble. They all do.

I don't look back. I don't need to. I can feel her behind me, hear the hesitant drag of her footsteps as we make our way outside. The chill of the evening air hits, but I don't slow down until we're far enough from the prying eyes of the staff quarters.

Then, I stop. Turn to face her.

"Where do you want to eat?" I ask, my voice as casual as if I were asking the time.

She freezes, her mouth opening and closing without a sound. The stunned look on her face almost makes me laugh.

"What?" she finally manages, her voice barely a whisper.

"Where do you want to eat?" I repeat, slower this time. I let the faintest hint of amusement creep into my tone, just enough to let her know I'm not asking to be difficult. I'm serious.

Her brow furrows, and she blinks, clearly struggling to process. "Uh…there's this little restaurant not far from here. It's…nice."

"Good." I give a single nod. "Let's go."

And just like that, I start walking again, leaving her to scramble to keep up. Whatever she thought this was going to be, it's not that.

I take the keys out of my pocket and hit the fob; the Audi flashes to life, unlocking the doors. I walk around to the passenger side and open the door for Luna. She's hesitating again, chewing on her bottom lip as I stand as patiently as I can until she finally gets in, and I close the door after her.

Once I'm in the car, we roll down the long driveway. In the distance, I can see my cousin Jack's house not far from mine. It's huge and dominating, just like him. We have never seen eye to eye, yet my father always seems to put us together on jobs.

We pass the opening gates and make our way into town. Luna doesn't speak a word until I pull up at the restaurant she had suggested.

"If you are going to fire me, you don't have to do it over dinner."

I ignore her remark and kill the engine. "Let's go," I say, and she gets out.

The dark, baggy clothes don't do her justice. Underneath the fabric, I know she's a knockout. The kind that could ruin a man— ruin me, if I let her.

Still, I can't stop looking. Her skin catches the faint glow of the streetlights, a soft shimmer on her collarbone where her hair brushes against it. She sucks her bottom lip between her teeth nervously, the action causing my cock to twitch.

The small diner at the corner is nothing fancy, but it's buzzing with patrons and just enough noise to drown out our words so no one can eavesdrop.

The waitress greets us with a tired smile and drops off menus. I don't even open mine. My attention stays locked on her, the way she chews the inside of her cheek while reading.

"You're staring," she says without looking up.

"Can't help it."

Her gaze flicks up, meeting mine, and for a moment, I swear she softens.

I lean back in my chair, watching her carefully. "So, tell me about yourself," I say, my voice steady but curious.

Her shoulders tense instantly, and I catch the flicker of hesitation in her eyes. She glances down, fiddling with her fingers. "What do you want to know?" she asks, her tone guarded. "It was all in my CV."

I let out a quiet chuckle, shaking my head. "Never got around to reading it," I admit, making a mental note that I will—later. I don't miss the way her lips press together, her expression unreadable.

She shrugs as if the answer is insignificant. "I'm an only child. Grew up in the heart of Dublin. Didn't really get along with my parents, so… I left. Started a new life down here. That's about it." Her words are clipped, rehearsed even, and there's something off in the way she avoids meeting my gaze.

I notice the tension still lingering in her shoulders, the slight twitch of her jaw. She's leaving something out—I can feel it. "And you've always wanted to be a cleaner?" I ask, my tone light, but there's an edge to the question.

Her head snaps up, and for a brief moment, I see the flicker of indignation in her eyes before she looks away. "I'm a qualified nurse," she says flatly.

A nurse? I wasn't expecting that. "Really?" The surprise in my voice is impossible to hide. "Then why aren't you working in a hospital?"

Her eyes narrow, her lips pressing into a thin line. "It's complicated," she mutters, her tone making it clear she doesn't want to elaborate.

Complicated. I don't buy it, but I let it slide for now. The truth will come out eventually—it always does. Still, the thought nags at me. If she's qualified, I could pull some strings, get her a position at any hospital she wants. But the idea of letting her go… it sits uncomfortably in my chest. I don't say anything, keeping that thought to myself.

Instead, she shifts the conversation, her voice softer now. "What about you?" she asks, her eyes finally meeting mine. There's curiosity there, but also caution, like she's unsure if she really wants to know the answer.

"Ask me any question; I'm an open book." I grin and open my arms wide for her.

The waitress appears. "Are you ready to order?"

I glance at Luna. "I'll have a vegetarian sandwich and a coffee."

The waitress scribbles the order down and glances at me.

"Just a coffee."

She gathers the menus and walks away.

"You aren't going to eat?" Luna asks, she's still so nervous, and I want nothing more than for her to relax.

"You aren't in trouble, and you aren't losing your job. So relax," I say.

"Then what are we doing here?" she glances around.

"Eating, well, you are eating, and I'm learning about you, Luna."

Her cheeks flush, and I see the slight lowering of her shoulders. "What about your family?" She finally asks.

What a loaded fucking question. "I have two brothers, Taghd and Niall. We all work together in the family business."

I'm waiting for her to ask what family business, but I'm sure she is fully aware we are mafia.

But then she tenses, glancing past me out the window.

Her hand moves to the edge of the table, fingers twitching like she's ready to bolt.

"What is it?" I ask, already turning to follow her line of sight.

She grabs my wrist, stopping me. "Don't."

The warning in her voice is clear, but so is the fear. I glance at her hand on mine, then back at her face.

"What is it?"

She exhales sharply, letting go. "He's here. Across the street."

I twist in my seat, ignoring her protests, and spot him instantly. The guy doesn't stand out much—a cheap leather jacket, a smirk that makes me want to break his jaw. He's flanked by two others, both trying too hard to look tough. I don't have to ask her who; this is clearly the boyfriend who uses her as a punching bag.

My fingers curl into fists. "Stay here."

"Wait, don't—"

I glance down at her. "He's your boyfriend?" I already know, but I just need to be one hundred percent certain. She gives a nod of her head.

"I promise I'll be gentle," I lie and get to my feet. Pushing through the front door.

The air outside is sharp, but I barely notice. My focus is on him. On the way his smug expression falters when he sees me coming across the road. The alleyway they are down is directly across from the restaurant.

I glance down the street, scanning the shadows that cling to the edges of the buildings. It's quiet—eerily quiet. No cameras, no witnesses, just the hum of the city far in the distance. Perfect. I take one last look around, ensuring there's no one here to see what's about to happen. My pulse is calm, steady, though the anger beneath my skin is anything but.

"You lost?" His voice cuts through the stillness as he steps forward, his cocky swagger as fake as the confidence in his eyes. Behind him, his friends linger, shifting uneasily. Smart of them to hang back.

"Not at all," I reply, my voice cool. My hands hang loosely at my sides, but every muscle in my body is coiled, ready.

He looks me up and down, his smirk widening. "You lookin' for something?" he says, his tone dripping with mockery.

I let the corner of my mouth curl into a grin, slow and deliberate. "Yeah," I say, taking a step closer, "and I think I found it."

His smirk falters, confusion flickering across his face. He

doesn't have time to figure it out. My fist connects with his jaw before he even sees it coming. The crack of bone echoes down the street, sharp and satisfying. He stumbles back, his hand flying to his face as blood trickles from the corner of his mouth. His friends lurch forward instinctively but stop themselves, uncertainty freezing them in place.

"You're gonna regret that," he spits, his voice dripping venom as he straightens, blood staining his teeth.

I pull the gun from my waistband, its weight grounding me in the moment. "No," I say, leveling my gaze at him, "you will."

His smirk vanishes as his eyes flick to the gun. His hands shoot up, palms out, the universal sign of surrender. "Whoa, man, come on," he stammers.

I slide the gun back into my waistband. "No fun in that, is there? You like hitting people, so here's your chance." I spread my arms wide, daring him. "Take a swing at me."

He hesitates, glancing at his friends, looking for reassurance. None comes. They stay rooted to the spot, just as useless as he is.

"What the fuck is wrong with you?" he mutters, shaking his head, but the fear in his eyes betrays him.

I step closer, my voice dropping to a deadly whisper. "You like hitting women, don't you? Makes you feel big, makes you feel in control. Well, here I am. Go on, big man, use me as your punching bag. What's the matter? Afraid?"

My grin widens, but there's no humor in it. Just sharp edges and promises of violence. He doesn't take the bait. He's too much of a coward for that. Instead, his hand darts to his pocket, and I catch the glint of a blade as he flicks it open.

Time slows. My gun is back in my hand before he even finishes the motion. His bravado crumbles instantly, replaced by something raw and primal—fear. Real fear. His eyes widen as I aim, my finger tightening on the trigger.

The shot shatters the stillness, loud and final. The bullet punches a clean hole through his forehead, and he collapses in a lifeless heap. His friends don't even scream. They just run, their footsteps fading into the distance.

I tuck the gun away, my movements methodical, unhurried. There's no need to rush. No one is coming—not yet. I turn and make my way back to the diner, the adrenaline humming low in my veins. My pulse is steady, my breathing even, as if I hadn't just ended a life.

Inside, she's frozen in place, her eyes locked on me, wide and unblinking. Her hands grip the edge of the table like it's the only thing keeping her upright. I slide into my seat, pick up my coffee, and take a slow sip, savoring the warmth.

Behind me, the murmurs start. People press against the windows, drawn by the sound of the gunshot, but none of it matters. The only thing that matters is her.

"You killed him," she whispers, her voice barely audible over the buzz of the diner.

I shrug, setting the cup back on the table. "He had it coming."

Her gaze doesn't waver, but there's something different now. Fear, yes, but something darker, something that flickers like a shadow at the edge of a flame. Intrigue, maybe. Or something far more dangerous.

I lean back in my chair, letting the silence stretch between us. "Still hungry?" I ask, my tone casual, like we're discussing the weather.

She doesn't answer. But she doesn't run, either.

And that tells me everything I need to know.

CHAPTER FIVE

O'REAGAN
AN CHLANN

Luna

I can't breathe. My chest tightens as though a vice is squeezing me, and the air feels too thick to pull into my lungs. My hands are trembling, my thoughts a whirlwind of disbelief, and something darker, something I'm afraid to name. He did that. He really did that.

Cian leans forward, his sharp gaze pinned on me. His voice is low, calm, like this is just another night for him. "I was sitting here the whole time with you," he says. "I never moved."

I nod, my head bobbing like it's not even mine. It's a lie—of course, it's a lie. But a part of me, the part that isn't screaming in terror, feels…relieved. What's wrong with me? What kind of person feels glad that their boyfriend is dead?

"Luna." His voice is softer now, a coaxing murmur. "It's time to go."

My eyes drop to his hand as he reaches for mine. The sleeve of his shirt—it's dark, but not dark enough to hide the spots of red splashed across it. Blood. That's blood. My stomach churns, but I don't pull away. I don't scream or cry, or do any of the things I should be doing. Instead, I let him take my hand, his fingers warm and steady around mine, and guide me to his car.

The door shuts with a muffled thunk, and I sink into the seat, staring straight ahead. The leather smells expensive, and it's eerily quiet like the car itself is complicit in keeping secrets. Cian pulls out his phone, the glow of the screen lighting his face in sharp angles. He's making a call, his voice low and clipped, but I can't focus on the words. They blur together, like static, and all I can hear is the bang of the gun. Over and over, it echoes in my mind. Is Mark really dead?

"Luna." Cian's voice slices through the fog, sharp and clear this time. I blink and look up. He's watching me again, his expression unreadable, but his eyes…there's something fierce in them, something that holds me captive.

"You can't go home," he says, and just like that, the weight of it all crashes down on me. This isn't a bad dream I'll wake up from. This is real.

"You killed him," I whisper, the words tasting foreign on my tongue.

"Yes." No hesitation. No remorse. Just that one word, delivered like it's a simple fact. Like it's nothing.

The car ride blurs after that. When I come back to myself, I'm standing in his house—his massive, immaculate house that smells like leather and wood polish. My legs feel shaky as he guides me upstairs to a sitting room. The fire crackles in the hearth, casting flickering shadows on the walls, and Cian moves with a quiet confidence, pouring a drink into a heavy crystal glass.

"Here," he says, pressing it into my hand. "Sip."

I don't argue. I lift the glass to my lips, the burn of the alcohol grounding me for a moment. When I lower it, he's kneeling in front of me, so close I can see the faint shadow of stubble along his jaw.

His hands rest lightly on his thighs, but his gaze is locked on mine, intense and unrelenting. "You're safe," he says softly, like he knows exactly what I need to hear. "I'll handle everything."

Safe. That word echoes in my mind, tangling with the other thoughts swirling around. I should feel anything but safe with him. But I can't take my eyes off him.

What is wrong with me?

I sit on the worn leather couch, the sting of alcohol still on my tongue. My hand trembles, the glass almost empty, as if nearly finishing it could erase what I just saw. Cian leans against the table, his dark brown eyes studying me, a soft chuckle escaping his lips. His laughter is light, almost boyish, and for a moment, it's hard to believe he's capable of…that.

But I know what I saw.

"Take another sip," he says, his tone low, steady. "It'll help with the shock."

The shock. As if alcohol can mend the crack running through my mind. I empty the glass anyway, feeling the burn sear down my throat. He smiles—not mockingly, but with some quiet understanding, like he's done this before. Maybe he has.

He takes the glass from me and rises to refill it, moving with a calmness that feels at odds with everything that just happened.

"Aren't you worried about getting in trouble?" I ask, my voice coming out smaller than I intended. It's not the first question I should ask, but it spills out anyway.

His back is to me as he pours, and his shoulders rise and fall in what might be a shrug. "That's not something you need to worry about."

The weight in his voice doesn't invite more questions, but I can't stop myself. "He wasn't always cruel." The words slip out, quieter than before. I barely hear myself, but Cian does.

He pauses, glancing over his shoulder, his gaze softer now, less dangerous.

"When he found me years ago, I was homeless." My voice breaks, and I hate how it makes me feel weak. "He took me in."

Cian hands me the refilled glass, his fingers brushing mine. He doesn't say anything right away; he just sinks back into the couch beside me. Too close. His presence is overwhelming, larger than life, but I don't feel afraid. Not of him.

"How did it start?" he asks, his tone gentler now, coaxing.

I hesitate, the words caught somewhere between my chest and throat. But I nod, taking another sip to steady myself. "Small things," I begin. "Telling me where I could go. Then what to wear." My face heats, shame bubbling up. "I shouldn't speak ill of the dead."

Cian's jaw tightens, his expression darkening, but he stays silent. Waiting.

"When did the hitting start?"

My breath catches, and I look down at the glass in my hands, watching the liquid tremble. "The first time was when I was still a nurse," I admit, the memory surfacing like a cold wave. "A male friend dropped me home after a late shift. He was convinced I'd cheated. I hadn't." The knot in my throat tightens, but I push the words out. "After that, he wouldn't let me go back to my job."

I shake my head, a bitter laugh escaping. "Things just got worse."

Cian doesn't say anything for a moment, and the silence stretches, heavy. Then he asks the question I've heard a hundred times before, the one that makes my chest feel like it's caving in.

"Why didn't you leave?"

I force myself to meet his gaze. Those dark eyes aren't judging me—they're steady, patient, like he already knows the answer but needs to hear it from me.

"Because I had nowhere to go."

The confession hangs between us, raw and unfiltered. Cian doesn't look away. He doesn't flinch or offer false comforts. He just stays there, grounding me, his presence a steady pulse in the chaos.

"I think something is wrong with me," I admit, the words tumbling out before I can stop them. Maybe it's the shock, maybe it's all the alcohol—or maybe it's the fact that I'm confessing to someone who can kill so easily. I'm not sure what makes me say it.

Cian's eyes flick to mine, sharp but not unkind. "Why?"

I hesitate, the truth clawing its way to the surface. "Because I have the urge to thank you… when I should be horrified."

The admission hangs in the air, heavy and twisted, and my gaze drops to the table. My voice feels distant, like I'm watching myself from the outside. What's wrong with me?

"You can thank me," Cian says, his tone low, almost a growl that reverberates in my chest.

I blink, startled by his response, but the words slip out anyway. "Thank you."

I frown as I speak, hating the way it feels. Knowing how messed up it is. My stomach knots, but Cian's grin only widens, sharp and wolfish, like he's amused by my conflict.

"You're very welcome," he says smoothly.

His grin fades, his expression darkening as he leans forward slightly. "Has anyone else ever hurt you?"

The question catches me off guard, and for a moment, my mind flashes to my parents. The fights, the neglect, the chaos of growing up in a house ruled by addiction. But they weren't cruel, not intentionally. They weren't like *him*. Would Cian even understand? Or would he see their failures as unforgivable and add their names to his list?

I shake my head, deciding some truths are better left buried.

Cian narrows his eyes, studying me like he's searching for cracks in my answer, but he doesn't push. Instead, he shifts gears, his voice calm and commanding. "You'll stay here for a few days."

He'd said this earlier, but it hadn't fully registered. Now it feels final, like a door quietly locking behind me.

"Won't someone be looking for me?" I ask, setting the second empty glass on the table. My head feels light, the alcohol a warm, numbing fog, but my stomach twists with unease.

Cian picks up my glass, his movements measured, almost too casual. "Like who?"

The question stops me cold. I don't have an answer, not a real

44

one. The truth is, no one's been looking out for me in a long time. But the Gardai—that's what they're supposed to do, isn't it?

"Like the Gardai," I say, the words trembling out. The moment they leave my lips, my stomach churns, regret pooling deep in my gut.

Cian doesn't flinch. He doesn't even hesitate. "They won't be looking for you."

His calm certainty makes my skin prickle. "How do you know that?" I ask, my voice barely above a whisper. For a moment, I don't think he'll answer.

Then he does.

"Because we own the Gardai."

His words slam into me, a cold, undeniable truth delivered without an ounce of apology. My pulse quickens, and my head spins—not from the alcohol this time, but from the realization of just how far his reach extends.

And yet, against all reason, I don't feel fear. What I feel is something much worse.

Relief.

CHAPTER SIX

O'REAGAN
AN CHLANN

Cian

I pace the length of the living room, each heavy step echoing off the hardwood floor. Her wide eyes follow me from where she's perched on the edge of the couch, her small frame almost swallowed by the dim light of the room. She looks nervous—like she's waiting for me to change my mind and tell her to leave.

"I'm telling you," I say, forcing the words out evenly, "you need to stay here for a few days. Just until things die down."

The truth is, it's not necessary. I've handled worse, and I know I could handle this without dragging her into it. But there's a pull I can't ignore, like an invisible thread tying me to her, winding tighter every time I look at her.

"And who decides when it 'dies down'?" she asks finally, her voice trembling slightly but defiant. "You?"

"Yes."

The word comes out clipped, sharper than I intend, and hangs in the air like an iron weight. Her hands tremble slightly, betraying the cracks in her armor. I let out a slow breath and walk to the chest behind the couch, pulling out a fur blanket. She flinches when I approach her, and I hate the fear in her eyes.

"Here," I mutter, draping the blanket across her lap. The soft fabric pools over her legs, but she doesn't relax. Not yet.

I sit down beside her, watching as her fingers twist and untwist the edge of the blanket. Her hands are small, delicate, but there's a rawness in the way she worries the fabric, like she's trying to unravel her own thoughts.

She probably thinks I'm no better than him—that I want to control her, cage her like some possession. The idea churns in my stomach, sour and wrong. If she were mine—and God, how badly I wish she were—I'd never hurt her. Never make her feel small or powerless.

I run a hand through my hair, exhaling slowly. "Look," I say, keeping my voice low, "I'm not trying to control you. I just... I need to keep you safe."

"Why?" she whispers, her voice so soft it barely registers. Her eyes meet mine, and there's a flicker of vulnerability there, like she's searching for a reason to trust me. "Why do you care?"

Because I can't stop. Because the thought of you in pain is enough to make my chest feel like it's caving in. But I can't say any of that—not yet.

"Because you're a part of my world now," I say instead. "And that makes it my problem."

Her gaze lingers on mine, her expression unreadable. For a moment, I think she's going to push back, argue. But then she nods, the motion slow and reluctant.

I lean back into the couch, but the tension in the room doesn't ease.

"So…what now?" she asks, her voice cutting through the quiet.

It's a good question—one I don't have an answer to. I glance at her again, taking in the way she's curled up, her shoulders hunched as if trying to shrink into herself.

I don't want her to feel small. Not here. Not with me.

"You hungry?" I ask, pushing myself to my feet.

She blinks, caught off guard. "You cook?"

I smirk, the corner of my mouth quirking up. "I didn't say that. But I can order takeout like a pro."

Her laugh is soft but real, and it cuts through the tension like a lifeline. "Takeout it is," she says, a faint smile tugging at her lips.

As I grab my phone, it buzzes in my hand. My father's name flashes on the screen, and the brief moment of levity evaporates. I already know what's coming.

"I'll be right back," I tell her, stepping into the hallway before answering.

"Yeah?"

"What the hell were you thinking?" His voice is a growl, low and dangerous, like a predator stalking its prey. "Do you have any idea what you've done?"

"He was hurting someone," I reply evenly, my grip tightening around the phone.

"That someone doesn't matter!" he snaps. "What matters is the fallout! You just shot the son of a man we've been working with for years. Do you understand the mess you've made?"

My jaw tightens. "I don't care. He deserved it."

"And if he retaliates? If this starts a war?"

"Then it starts a war," I say coldly. "I'm not apologizing for protecting her."

There's a beat of silence, heavy and suffocating. Then he asks, "And who exactly is she?"

I glance toward the living room door. I can still see her in my mind—curled up on the couch, clutching the blanket like it's the only thing keeping her grounded.

"She's my girlfriend," I lie, the words slipping out before I can stop them. The truth would sound ridiculous even to me.

My father exhales sharply, his disdain cutting through the line. "Since when do you care about anyone but yourself?"

The words hit harder than I want to admit, but I keep my voice steady. "Since now."

His silence is louder than his anger. "Fix this, son. Or I will."

The line goes dead, but the weight of his threat lingers. Fix this. As if it's that simple.

When I step back into the living room, she's asleep. Her small frame is curled into the corner of the couch, her head resting on her knees. The blanket has slipped off her shoulders, and her breathing is soft, steady.

For a moment, I just stand there watching her. She looks so fragile, like a doll that's been tossed aside too many times. But I know better. There's steel in her. Enough to survive him. Enough to survive this.

I step closer, pulling the blanket back over her shoulders. She stirs slightly but doesn't wake, and I sink into the chair across from her, my gaze never leaving her face.

It doesn't matter what it costs. It doesn't matter how many enemies I have to face.

No one is hurting her again. Not now. Not ever.

A part of me wants to wake her up right now, shake her out of that fragile sleep, and demand answers about her boyfriend. Who he was. Whether she knew he might be tied to a gang.

The idea twists in my chest. Luna doesn't strike me as someone who gets tangled up with men like that—men like me. She's too soft around the edges, too...genuine. But then again, she must have known I was Mafia when she took the job. She walked into my world willingly.

Why?

I rake a hand through my hair, frustration simmering beneath the surface. I need to know more about him. About her.

His body's probably already in the ground, courtesy of my cleanup crew. Any footage from the area? Erased. My men are combing through his circle now, hunting down anyone close to him. None of them will see tomorrow's sunrise. As for the witnesses in the café, the Gardai will handle them. They're in my pocket, and they know better than to dig too deep.

Normally, I'd never be this reckless. I don't kill without planning every angle, every consequence. But back in that café, the second I saw the fear in her eyes, every shred of control burned to ash. The fucker pulled a knife, and it was over. It might as well have been self-defense.

That's what I'll tell myself, anyway.

I glance at her again, curled up on the couch, her breathing soft and steady. The sight of her stirs something in me, but only for a moment.

Leaving her there, I head to the bathroom. The shirt I'm wearing has blood on the cuffs—his blood—and it needs to go. Stripping it off, I step into the shower, letting the scalding water beat down on me. The heat doesn't wash away the tension, but it dulls the edge enough to think straight.

When I'm done, I toss the shirt into the fireplace in my office. The fabric curls and blackens, the flames licking away the evidence until it's nothing but ash. Cleaned up and dressed in black pants and a sweater, I feel like myself again—controlled, calculated.

By the time I return to the living room, she's still asleep, her soft breathing filling the silence. I don't wake her yet. Instead, I pull out my phone and place an order with the local Chinese restaurant. I don't know what she likes, so I order everything: sweet and sour chicken, fried rice, spring rolls, noodles, and half the menu for good measure.

When the food arrives, I tell the house staff to leave for the night. The place feels too full, too loud with them here. I keep only the security team on site—they'll stay out of sight unless I need them.

The dining room feels cavernous once it's quiet, the polished table gleaming under the soft light. I set up the food, arranging the containers like I'm hosting a dinner party instead of trying to win over a woman I've just dragged into my world.

Once it's all set up, I return upstairs to Luna. She stirs, a soft rustle of movement. I step into the doorway, leaning casually against the frame.

"Come with me," I say, my voice gentle but firm.

Her eyes flutter open, hazy with sleep, and she blinks up

52

at me. For a moment, she looks confused, vulnerable, like she's forgotten where she is. Then the memory clicks, and she pulls the blanket tighter around her shoulders.

She doesn't argue. Doesn't question. She just nods and rises to her feet, her movements slow and cautious. I step aside, giving her space, and lead the way to the dining room.

When we enter, her eyes widen slightly at the spread of food laid out on the table. The faintest hint of a smile tugs at her lips, and I feel a small flicker of satisfaction.

"I didn't know what you liked," I admit, gesturing to the feast. "So I got a little of everything."

Her gaze flickers to mine, and for the first time since this whole mess started, she doesn't look afraid. "A little?" she murmurs, her voice tinged with amusement.

"Okay, a lot," I concede, pulling out a chair for her.

She sits down, her movements still tentative, and I take the seat across from her. The silence stretches between us, heavy with everything unspoken.

For now, I let it be. There will be time for answers later. Tonight, I just need her to eat. To feel safe. To start trusting me— even if I don't deserve it yet.

For someone so small, she eats like she hasn't had a proper meal in days. And I can't stop watching her. Every movement, every bite—it's hypnotic. The way she tilts her head slightly when she's deciding what to try next, or how her lips curve ever so slightly in satisfaction when she finds something she likes. She's mesmerizing, and I know I should stop staring, but I can't.

"I could never eat this kind of food when…"

She trails off, her voice faltering, and her gaze drops to her plate. She doesn't need to finish for me to understand. Mark. It always comes back to him. My jaw tightens at the thought of him controlling something as simple and basic as what she eats. It's sick.

"Eat whatever you want," I say, forcing my voice to stay even. I bite back the anger threatening to edge into my tone. I don't want her to think I'm mad at her, but the thought of him dictating her life like that makes my blood boil.

Her fork hovers over her plate as she glances up at me, her eyes searching mine for something—permission, maybe, or reassurance. I hold her gaze, willing her to see that I mean it.

She pauses again, her brow furrowing. "Why aren't you eating?"

For a second, I'm caught off guard by the question. It's such a simple thing, but the way she asks it—it's not just about the food. It's about her need to feel normal, to share this moment with someone.

I smile, the corners of my mouth lifting, and reach for my plate. "You're right," I say lightly, piling some of the food onto it. "I should eat."

Her lips twitch into a small, genuine smile, and something warm unfurls in my chest, spreading through me like a quiet fire. It's startling, this need to make her happy, to see her smile again.

I take a bite of the sweet and sour chicken, and when I glance back up at her, she's watching me now, her expression softer than before. For the first time, the tension between us feels less like a barrier and more like a thread—fragile but something I want to hold onto.

We eat in silence for a while, but it doesn't feel heavy or strained. It's a strange kind of peace, and I find myself wanting it to last. Wanting her to stay in this moment, where she feels safe enough to eat as much as she wants and doesn't have to worry about anything else.

If I have anything to say about it, this is how it will always be for her from now on. No one controlling her. No one hurting her. Just freedom.

CHAPTER SEVEN

O'REAGAN
AN CHLANN

Luna

I wake to the aroma of freshly brewed coffee and something else—eggs, maybe bacon. For a moment, I forget where I am. The room is too big, too luxurious for my modest apartment, and then it hits me. I'm still here, in his house, wrapped in his world. A world that I know I don't belong to.

The night before, after we finished the Chinese food, he led me to a room that took my breath away. The bed alone looked like it belonged in a palace, draped in soft, white linens with gold accents. The furnishings were rich and so far removed from anything I'd ever experienced.

"You'll stay here," he said, his tone firm but not unkind. "The staff won't be in tomorrow. I figured you'd want some space."

That was a relief. The idea of being scrutinized by housekeepers or cooks who might wonder why someone like me was staying in a house like this made my stomach churn. Especially with Sara. I'm sure she has been telling everyone that I left with Cian. The look on her face had told me she had thought I was in trouble; at that moment, so had I.

"Thank you," I murmur, though gratitude felt inadequate for everything I was processing.

"Some clothes will arrive for you tomorrow," he added almost casually.

I straightened at that, frowning. "I don't need that. I can just go back home and grab some things."

The shift in his demeanor was instant. The warmth in his expression gave way to something darker, colder.

"No," he said sharply. "It's best you don't."

His tone brooked no argument, and I wasn't brave enough to push further. But the command lingered with me, unsettling.

Later, as I lay in the enormous bed, trying to calm my thoughts, I saw the missed call on my phone. Becca. A pang of guilt hit me. She must be worried. Tomorrow, I promised myself. Tomorrow, I'll call her back and try to explain…something. Though what, I still wasn't sure.

Sliding out of the plush bed, I stretch, the silk of the borrowed pajama set cool against my skin. It feels indulgent, wearing something so expensive that isn't even mine. I pad toward the door and down the hall, the soft sounds of a distant radio murmuring through the house.

The kitchen is bathed in golden morning light, and he's there, standing at the stove. His broad shoulders are relaxed, the sleeves of his shirt rolled up to his elbows. The sight is disarming— domestic, almost. He glances back at me, a slight smirk playing on his lips.

"Morning," he says, his voice low and warm.

"Morning," I reply, feeling awkward and unsure. It's not like we're just two regular people sharing breakfast.

He gestures to the counter. "Sit. Coffee?"

I nod, sinking onto one of the barstools. The counter is cold under my fingertips, a stark contrast to the warmth he exudes even from across the room. He moves with a casual confidence, pouring me a cup and sliding it in front of me.

"Thanks," I say, wrapping my hands around the mug. The first sip is heaven, rich and strong, and I let it settle me.

"You slept okay?" he asks, his tone conversational, but there's an edge of genuine concern there.

I hesitate before answering. "Yeah. Better than I thought I would."

He nods, turning some bacon. The act is so ordinary it's almost jarring. This is the same man who, just days ago, shot someone in the face without flinching. The memory tightens my chest. The news hasn't let me forget it—flashes of the scene replaying every time I catch a headline.

But here, in this moment, he doesn't seem like that man. He seems like someone else entirely. Someone who, against all logic, makes me feel safe. It's confusing, infuriating even, how those two versions of him can coexist.

"What's going on in that head of yours?" His voice pulls me from my thoughts. He's watching me now, leaning casually against the counter, the bacon forgotten for the moment.

I shrug, trying to play it off. "Just... wondering how you make your coffee taste this good."

59

He chuckles, a deep, genuine sound that makes my stomach flutter. "Trade secret. You'll have to stick around if you want to figure it out."

It's a joke, but the words hang in the air, heavy with implication. Stick around. Like this is something that could last. The thought terrifies me as much as it tempts me.

I take another sip, avoiding his gaze. "What's the plan for today?" I ask, steering the conversation somewhere safer.

He raises an eyebrow. "Planning to run?"

"I didn't say that."

"No, but you thought it," he says, his tone unreadable. "And you wouldn't be wrong to. It'd be smart, even. Safer."

I flinch, the honesty in his words cutting deeper than I expected. "I don't know what I'm doing," I admit softly, setting the mug down.

"You don't have to," he says simply. "Not right now."

It's an answer that offers no clarity, but maybe that's the point. Maybe there isn't any clarity to be found in this…whatever this is. My mind spins, torn between the undeniable pull I feel toward him and the cold, hard reality of what he is. What he does.

"I saw the news again last night," I say suddenly, the words slipping out before I can stop them. "They showed the scene. The blood."

He stiffens, his expression hardening just enough to remind me of whom I'm talking to.

"And?" he prompts, his voice steady but guarded.

"And I don't know how to reconcile that with…this." I gesture vaguely around the kitchen.

His eyes meet mine, unflinching. "You think I'm a monster?"

The question is like a punch to the gut. Do I? My mind flashes to the sound of the gunshot, the way he'd looked afterward—calm, composed, like it was just another day. But then I see him here, offering me coffee, making bacon, watching me with a softness that feels so at odds with everything I know about him.

"I don't know what to think," I admit, my voice barely above a whisper.

For a moment, he doesn't say anything. Then he sighs, running a hand through his hair. "I won't apologize for what I've done," he says. "It's who I am. But that doesn't mean it's all I am."

His words hang in the air, heavy and unshakable. I want to believe him. I want to believe that there's more to him than the violence and the darkness. But wanting doesn't make it true.

Still, as I sit there, watching him flip the bacon onto a plate and set it in front of me with a small smile, I can't deny the way my heart skips a beat. And that, more than anything, terrifies me.

I'm midway through my coffee, savoring the last bite of crispy bacon, when Cian leaves briefly. He arrives back into the kitchen. "Your new clothes have arrived. They're up in your room."

"I…" My voice falters. "Cian, I can't keep accepting all of this. It's too much."

His mouth tilts into a faint smirk. "You'll get over it," he says, dismissing my concern with a wave of his hand. "Go shower, get dressed. I have something I want to show you."

"What is it?" I ask, my curiosity piqued, but he shakes his head.

"Just do as I say. You'll like it."

I want to argue, but I don't. Instead, I drain the last of my coffee and finish the bacon, savoring the care someone else has put into making sure I'm fed. Being taken care of like this is something I could get used to, even if it's all temporary.

When I reach my room, my steps falter at the sight of the bed. Stacks of clothes—more than I could have imagined—are laid out neatly. Sweaters in soft fabrics, trousers that look tailored, and even shoes lined up against the wall. My face burns when my gaze lands on a small black lingerie set nestled among the rest. The delicate lace feels like a mocking whisper of indulgence as I pick it up. My throat tightens.

This is too much.

Still, my fingers trail over the cream sweater and black trousers, and I know they're exactly my size. It's surreal, the precision of it all. With a shake of my head, I grab the clothes and head for the shower.

The water races across my skin, a little too hot. It's a grounding heat, a small punishment for letting myself be swept into this strange, pampered life. As I towel off and glance around the bathroom, another wave of surprise washes over me. A new toothbrush, a hairbrush, creams, and even perfumes are arranged neatly on the counter.

My fingers hesitate over a glass bottle of perfume. I'm tempted to spritz it just to know what kind of scent Cian picked out. Instead, I stare at myself in the mirror, my damp hair clinging to my neck, the cream sweater now snug against my skin.

This isn't me. This polished woman with expensive clothes and perfectly curated toiletries can't be me.

"I can't do this," I whisper, the words bouncing back at me.

But the mirror doesn't argue. My reflection stares back, almost daring me. Why not? Don't I deserve a break? After everything—after Mark?

A part of me reasons I can pretend, just for a little while. Pretend this is my life, that I'm someone worthy of all of this—just for now.

I pick up my phone and hesitate. Texting Becca feels like a coward's move, but I'm not brave enough to call. I type quickly, crafting an excuse that's barely a lie.

Staying over at Cian's for a bit. Lots of work to do. Nice to get away from Mark.

I hover over the send button. She'll have questions. The news hasn't mentioned Mark's name, at least not yet. But I can't think about that right now. My finger presses send before I can second-guess it further.

When I go downstairs, the first thing I notice is Cian's suit. He looks effortlessly handsome, the crisp cut of the fabric framing his broad shoulders perfectly. He's snacking on peanuts from a bowl, his movements slow and deliberate, as though he has all the time in the world.

He glances up when he hears my steps. "Ready?"

For a moment, I just stand there, unsure how to respond. Everything feels so surreal—his calm, the luxury surrounding me, the tension simmering in the air between us.

I nod, even though I'm not sure I am. "Yeah. I'm ready."

CHAPTER EIGHT

O'REAGAN
AN CHLANN

Cian

Luna slides into the passenger seat, her hands trembling as she fumbles with the seatbelt. She seems nervous.

The engine hums to life, and she jumps slightly at the sound. Without a word, I reach across, my hand touches her thigh.

"It's okay. You have nothing to worry about."

She nods, her focus on my hand, the warmth of her skin under me has my hand lingering for a moment longer than is actually necessary, I pull back, and shift the gears, and drive off the property. Luna is looking out the window, but I still catch the glow on her cheeks.

The drive to the nursing home isn't long. It's one of the private ones, tucked away in the countryside, with the kind of reputation that speaks for itself—top-tier doctors, attentive nurses, and a sense of warmth that doesn't feel manufactured. I made sure of that personally. My mum's mother—my nan—deserves nothing less.

Today's visit is twofold. For one, it's Thursday, and Thursday means Nan. Always has. But I'm also thinking about Luna. This place could be perfect for her. She's been searching for work that means something, and this feels like a win-win. At least, that's my logic. Whether Luna sees it that way? We're about to find out.

The car rolls to a stop at the gated entrance, and I lean out to sign us in. Beyond the gates, small houses dot the perimeter like a quaint little village, their gardens neat and orderly. The main building looms ahead, where Nan lives. A familiar sight. Comforting, in a way.

When I pull up and kill the engine, I glance at Luna. Her expression is...unreadable. She's been quiet the entire drive, but now her brow furrows as she looks at the nursing home.

"A nursing home?" she asks, her voice tinged with surprise. Not judgment, but close enough to make me defensive.

"Yeah," I reply, keeping my tone even. "My nan lives here. I visit her every Thursday."

Her eyes meet mine, and something shifts. The surprise fades, replaced by something softer, something... unexpected. It's like she's seeing me differently, like she's peeling back another layer. I clear my throat and push open the door before I can analyze it further.

Out of the trunk, I grab the bouquet of bright carnations—Nan's favorite—and a box of Maltesers. The same chocolates I've brought her every Thursday for years. Routine. Predictable. But it matters to her, and that's what counts.

Luna steps out of the car, still watching me. She doesn't say anything, but I can feel the weight of her gaze as I close the trunk and head toward the entrance. Maybe she's waiting for me to explain more, to add something deeper to my simple Thursday tradition. But some things don't need words.

"Coming?" I ask, tilting my head toward the entrance.

She nods, her lips twitching into a faint smile. "Yeah. Let's meet your nan."

I guide Luna through the double oak doors of the nursing home, the scent of lavender and freshly baked cookies greeting us like an embrace. This place isn't just a nursing home; it's a sanctuary. The floors gleam, reflecting the soft, golden light streaming in through floor-to-ceiling windows. Staff in crisp, white uniforms move gracefully, smiling and greeting residents like family. The air hums with serenity. It's exactly how it should be.

"Morning, Cian," Jessie, one of the nurses in her late 50's greets me with a warm smile and open arms. I accept the embrace before planting a kiss on her forehead.

"She's all revved up to see you." She states when I release her.

Jessie glances at Luna, her brows rising. "You brought a friend."

"My girlfriend," I answer, and Luna stiffens beside me. I haven't explained to her that my father believes she's my girlfriend. I use the opportunity to reach across and take Luna's hand in mine.

Jessie's smile radiates. "Aren't you a lucky man?"

"That I am." I smile back.

"Enjoy your visit," Jessie says to Luna who manages to just nod.

"I'll explain on the way back, but in front of my nan you are my girlfriend," I tell Luna as we make our way through the airy lobby. She hasn't withdrawn her hand from mine, and I take that as a good sign.

Once again, she just nods but looks around her with wide eyes taking in everything—the plush armchairs, the carefully tended plants, the cheerful murmur of voices from a nearby common area.

"It's beautiful," she finally says, her voice soft. She looks at me, her brows furrowed just slightly, as if trying to reconcile the man she knows with the one who brought her here or the one who is telling people she's his girlfriend. "I didn't expect this."

"What? Thought I'd dump her in some run-down place?" I smirk, but there's no edge to it. I stop at a doorway and knock lightly before pushing it open. "I'd never do that to her."

Inside, my nan sits at a small table, a deck of cards already laid out in front of her. Her silver hair is neatly pinned back, and her eyes light up when she sees me.

"Cian!" she exclaims, her voice warm and strong despite her age. "You finally came to visit your old gran."

"Old? Never," I tease, releasing Luna's hand and crossing the room to kiss her cheek. She laughs, swatting at me lightly before her gaze shifts to Luna.

"And who is this lovely young lady?"

"Gran, this is Luna, my girlfriend," I say, stepping aside so they can see each other properly. "Luna, this is the woman who taught me everything I know about winning at cards. Be warned."

Luna smiles, a little shy but charmed. "It's nice to meet you, Ma'am."

"Oh, none of that Ma'am nonsense," Nan says, waving her hand. "Call me Eileen. Now, come sit. Let's see who has finally captured Cian's heart."

Luna hesitates as we step into the room, her unsure gaze flicking to me. I nod slightly, a silent reassurance, like telling her, *Just play along. It's fine.* Reluctantly, she sits down across from my nan, who's already beaming as if Luna is the best surprise she's had in weeks.

The moment Luna settles, Nan reaches out and takes her hands, her frail fingers clasping Luna's firmly but gently. Her smile widens, her eyes lighting up in that way only Nan can manage.

"She's pretty," Nan says, her tone full of approval as her gaze shifts to me. "Very pretty."

I shrug off my suit jacket and drape it over the back of a chair, letting a faint smile touch my lips. "I know," I answer, my voice calm but certain. It's not just a polite agreement—it's the truth. Luna isn't just pretty; she's stunning, the kind of woman who could silence a room without even trying.

Nan doesn't miss a beat. Her frail hands tighten on Luna's. "She's got soft hands," she says, marveling at them like they're something precious. I sit down with them, letting the warmth of the moment settle over the room.

"She's a nurse," I add smoothly.

Nan's jaw drops slightly, her eyes wide with admiration. "A nurse?" she repeats, her voice reverent, as if Luna's profession has elevated her to sainthood. "You have kind eyes, Luna. Being a nurse suits you."

Luna flushes, a soft pink blooming on her cheeks. "Thank you," she murmurs, her voice small but sincere. For the first time, I catch a glimpse of a real, unguarded smile from her—a soft, genuine curve of her lips that makes her look even more beautiful.

Nan releases Luna's hands then, leaning back in her chair with a tilt of her head, her sharp gaze darting between us. "So," she begins, mischief sparkling in her eyes, "how did you two meet?"

I answer before Luna has a chance to overthink it. "At a restaurant," I say easily, letting the lie roll off my tongue like second nature. "One look, and I knew I had to have her."

Nan laughs a delighted, warm sound that echoes through the room. "You always go after whatever you want, Cian," she says, reaching across the table to pat my cheek. Her hand lingers for a moment, and her expression softens. "That's why I love you."

"Because I'm your favorite grandson," I tease, smirking at her.

She chuckles, shaking her head slightly, but her eyes betray her. It's true, even if she'd never say it out loud. Niall and Tadgh don't visit her much—not like I do. They're too busy, too wrapped up in their own lives. But Nan has always held a special place in my heart, and I like to think I've done the same for her.

Her gaze lingers on me for a moment longer before she turns back to Luna, a sly smile playing on her lips. "You've got your hands full with this one, my dear," she says, her voice warm but teasing.

Luna glances at me, and for a moment, there's something in her expression—something almost amused, almost...content. She doesn't answer Nan, but that soft smile lingers.

"Let's play cards." I declare picking up the deck and shuffling them like Nan taught me.

We sit down, and for the next hour, the three of us play cards. Nan is as sharp as ever, laughing at our missteps and offering Luna tips with the kind of warmth only she can manage. Luna, for her part, is a quick study, her competitive streak coming out in a way that makes Nan laugh even harder. I mostly watch, enjoying the rare sight of two women getting along so effortlessly.

After a while, a staff member comes by with a tray of tea and a plate of tiny, sugar-dusted rose-shaped pastries. Gran insists we try them, and I'm reminded again why I made sure she ended up in a place like this. Every detail, down to the food, is perfect.

Luna bites into one, her eyes widening in delight. "These are incredible."

"Only the best here," I say, leaning back in my chair. "That's why I thought of you."

She blinks, confused. "Me?"

"You'd make a great nurse here. It's well-paid, low-pressure. Every staff member gets plenty of time with their patients. None of that assembly-line care you've told me about. You'd fit right in."

Luna stares at me, her expression unreadable. For a moment, I think she's going to laugh or brush it off, but instead, she sets her teacup down carefully.

"You…you'd help me get a job here?" Her voice is quiet, as if she's afraid to hope.

"Of course," I say, meeting her gaze. "If you want it, it's yours. You deserve better than what you've got now, Luna."

She looks down at her hands, twisting them together. I can see the wheels turning in her head, the way she's trying to reconcile this offer with whatever doubts she carries. Finally, she looks up, her eyes a little too bright.

"I…I'll think about it," she says, her voice trembling slightly.

"That's all I ask," I reply, keeping my tone light even as relief

71

floods through me. I don't want to push her, but I hope she sees what I see: a chance for something better.

Nan claps her hands, breaking the moment. "Enough serious talk. Let's see if Luna can beat me one more time before you two leave."

Luna laughs, and just like that, the heaviness lifts. We dive back into the game, but my mind lingers on her expression, the way her guard slipped just enough for me to see the vulnerability beneath. She'll think about it, she said. I'll make sure she knows she's worth saying yes.

CHAPTER NINE

O'REAGAN
AN CHLANN

Cian

Jessie arrives in the room, and as always, takes the flowers I bought and places them in a fresh vase, she watches us playing cards as she moves around the room. Time slips by, and I know it's time to go.

I hate leaving, but I know it's Nan's nap time. The last thing I want is to exhaust her. Brushing a kiss against her forehead, I whisper, "I'll see you next Thursday."

She smiles warmly, her gaze shifting to Luna. "I hope you come by again."

Luna leans in, her smile soft and fond. "I promise I will."

Before I can step away, Nan pulls Luna into a hug, surprising both of us. "I might see a lot more of you if you take that job Cian offered," she says, a twinkle in her eye as she winks at me. Always the matchmaker, my nan.

Luna blushes, and I chuckle softly as I slip my suit jacket back on. Reaching for her hand, I feel her fingers slide effortlessly into mine as if they belong there. We make our way out to the car, the quiet of the nursing home grounds settling over us.

Once we're inside, Luna tilts her head, a playful glint in her eyes. "So, I'm your girlfriend now?" Her tone is light, teasing, but there's something underneath it I can't quite place.

I don't answer right away. Instead, I lean back against the seat, my mind shifting to something darker. I don't start the car. Instead, I glance at her, my expression serious. "My father called," I begin, my voice low, almost reluctant. "It's about Mark."

Her body tenses immediately, the name struck a chord like I knew it would. I hate bringing him up, but it's necessary. "Did you know he was part of a gang?" I ask, watching her closely, looking for any flicker of recognition.

She shakes her head, her lips pressing into a thin line. "No," she admits, her voice quiet but steady. "He never told me what he was doing. I was always on a need-to-know basis. But deep down...I knew he wasn't making his money legitimately."

I nod, my jaw tightening. "Well, he was part of a gang," I confirm. "And now they want retribution for what happened. His father—he wants you."

Luna's face drains of color, her hand trembling as she clutches her seatbelt. "His father?" she whispers, her voice barely audible. "I've only met him a few times, but he was..." She trails off, her brows furrowing as if she's dredging up memories she'd rather forget. "I didn't get a good feeling about him."

I start the car, gripping the wheel tightly. "Well, he blames you for Mark's death," I say flatly. "So, now he wants you."

Her hand shakes as she fastens her seatbelt, her knuckles

white. The silence between us grows heavy, and then she asks, her voice so soft I almost miss it, "Are you going to hand me over?"

The question stuns me. My head snaps toward her, my eyes narrowing. "No," I reply, my tone sharp but sincere. "The only way I could protect you was by saying you were my girlfriend."

She nods slowly, her expression unreadable. But then I catch it—a flicker of something in her eyes. Disappointment? Hurt? I can't tell, and before I can address it, she turns her gaze out the window.

The rest of the drive is quiet, the tension between us thick. I don't push her to talk, and she doesn't offer anything. Her silence gnaws at me, but for now, I let it be.

Once I pull up to the house, I'm not ready to get out. "I know I didn't ask your permission to say you are my girlfriend, but it was the only thing I could think of at the time to keep you safe."

Luna removes her belt and pivots towards me. "I'm still unsure why you are doing all of this, but thank you, and I don't mind being your girlfriend." The way she says the last part has me chuckling.

"It's not too much of a burden on you?" I ask.

She shakes her head. "Not at all." There is longing in her voice and my gaze dips to her wet lips. She hasn't moved and I inch closer to her, I wait and when she doesn't recoil, I move a bit closer. "If we are going to pretend to be dating, we should at least kiss," I say.

Luna swallows and wets her lips again. "That makes sense," her voice is small.

I reach out and take her face in my hand. Her skin is soft

and warm against my palm. Her wide hazel eyes are open and vulnerable at this moment, and I have the most corrupt thoughts. My cock twitches at the thought of burying myself in her, but I know I need to take things slow with her, and slow is never a pace I move at.

My lips brush hers gently and she takes a large breath of air; I give her a moment to stop this because if I continue, I know I won't be able to stop wanting her. She doesn't pull away; she does the opposite. Her lips press firmly and hungrily against mine, her hands reaching up and gripping my shoulders.

She tastes of coffee and something sweet, her mouth is warm as I slip my tongue between her lips and she groans into my mouth. My cock twitches again, my hands tighten on her face, tilting her head to give me more access to her perfect mouth. A light from inside the house seems to grow brighter behind my eyelids, alerting me to someone's presence. I break the kiss and look away from a dazed Luna, only to see my father standing at the front door.

Fuck.

"Everything okay?" Luna asks.

"That's my dad. We'd better go in."

We get out of the car, and my dad disappears back inside the house. This isn't good if he's making house calls.

We step inside, and the tension snaps taut when I see my father waiting in the living room. His face is set in grim lines, his arms crossed over his chest.

"What's going on?" I ask, my voice sharper than I intended.

"You took her to see your grandmother?" My father says and Luna seems to shrink back behind me.

I reach out and take her hand in mine. "Yes." I don't bother asking him how he knows; one is that I go every Thursday and secondly, I'm always being watched.

"How was she?" he asks while rubbing his jaw.

"Maybe you should visit her," I say back. He was never a fan of my grandmother, some old beef that they didn't quite squash about him dating my mum when they were younger.

He takes another look at Luna and my fingers instantly tighten around hers, letting her know she's safe.

My father is old school mafia, and I know he can come across as extremely intimidating, but I want Luna to feel safe.

"This is Luna, whom I told you about, my girlfriend." I tug Luna gently, so she comes to stand beside me.

"It's nice to meet you." My father clears the distance and holds out his hand.

Luna glances at me before she takes it and gives his hand a light shake.

He nods at her before his focus is back on me. "The gang wants retribution. They want the girl back." His gaze flickers to Luna, then back to me. "I told them no."

My stomach knots, but I nod. "Good."

"You understand what that means?" he asks, his tone hard.

I meet his eyes. "Yeah. It means we fight."

He nods once, approval mingled with resignation. "Okay, so now we fight this war. Do you understand?"

"I do." My voice doesn't waver. I can't afford it.

His gaze shifts to Luna again, softer this time, before he looks back at me. "Don't leave the house. They'll have shooters ready to take you out. Sit tight until you hear from me."

"Got it."

He doesn't linger. He turns on his heel and walks out, the door shutting behind him with a finality that echoes through the house.

Luna stands frozen, her face pale. I step closer, placing a hand on her arm.

"You'll be okay," I say. "I'll make sure of it."

She nods, but her eyes stay on the door, as if expecting it to burst open any second.

CHAPTER TEN

O'REAGAN
AN CHLANN

Luna

The air feels heavier tonight, like the world knows something is about to crack open. I pace the length of the living room, biting my thumbnail and trying—and failing—to make sense of the storm inside me. Sara is back at work and each time she passes the living room that I have stayed in, I quickly turn away so I don't meet her questioning gaze. She doesn't seem to dare enter. Right now, I don't even know what to say to anyone. I've texted Becca to tell her I'm still staying over at Cian's but she sent back emojis of love-hearts making me smile for a brief moment.

Cian's face flashes in my mind—the way he had held my hand in front of his father, the flash of intensity in his eyes when he was trying to protect me. He's trying so hard to protect me, but I know I've brought this all upon myself, and hearing his father say they were going to war makes me feel sick to my stomach.

I drag a hand through my hair and sink onto the couch. "Get it together, Luna," I mutter. But even as the words leave my mouth, my heart pulls in two directions. One part wants to surrender, to admit that I'm falling for Cian—falling hard. The other screams at me to remember who I am. I'm his cleaner who wants to stay in this lavish life.

My ex's father, Richard Fitzsimons, is a name that makes me curl in on myself. I've met him a few times and each time I wanted to run away from him. I had the feeling he wasn't a good man, but to find out he's the leader of some powerful gang is frightening, and the fact he wants me, like he knows I'm the reason his son is dead, makes him all the more terrifying. But the thought that he is planning to attack Cian has me knowing I need to do something.

I need to ring him. My phone sits on the coffee table, mocking me with its silence. Call him. Try to reason with him. I already know I can't, I don't have the man's number. I could go back to the apartment and find Mark's second phone that he keeps along the side of his recliner in the living room.

Cian was warned by his father not to leave but only an hour after his father left, he promised he would be back shortly and warned me to stay here.

But, I can't sit around and do nothing.

The staff kitchen smells faintly of coffee and bleach, a clash of the comforting and the clinical. Sara is leaning against the counter, scrolling through her phone with one hand while the other cradles a steaming mug. I hesitate in the doorway, my hand tightening around the edge of the frame. She hasn't noticed me yet. Good. I need a moment to piece together the lie—something plausible, easy to say, easier to believe.

"Sara?" I step inside, schooling my face into something neutral. Friendly, even.

She looks up, her brow lifting as if she's surprised to see me, fair enough I have been avoiding her. "What's up?"

"Can I borrow your car?" The words tumble out too quickly, too rehearsed. I force a small laugh to soften the urgency in my voice. "Just for a quick run. I'll have it back before your shift ends."

Sara straightens, her eyes narrowing slightly. "Why? You staying around here or something?"

"Oh, yeah." I wave a hand, dismissing the question before it can take root. "Had a serious leak at my place. Cian…" I pause, my stomach twisting as I say his name. "Cian was kind enough to let me crash for a bit while it gets sorted."

The lie slips off my tongue with alarming ease, the practiced skill of someone who's had to lie before—too many times. Sara doesn't respond immediately, just studies me with a look that says she's trying to decide whether I'm full of it. I feel the weight of her scrutiny, the pause stretching too long.

Finally, she sighs and pulls her keys from her pocket, tossing them onto the counter between us. "My shift ends in two hours," she says, her voice carrying a warning.

"I'll be back by then," I promise, snatching the keys before she can change her mind. "Thanks, Sara. I owe you."

She doesn't reply, just takes a sip of her coffee, her eyes lingering on me as I leave. My heart doesn't slow until I'm in the car, gripping the steering wheel like it might steady me.

The drive to the apartment feels longer than it is. Every glance in the rearview mirror sends a spike of paranoia through me. I'm not being followed—I've checked enough times to be sure—but the fear doesn't care about logic. It sits heavy in my chest, a constant companion.

When I finally pull up outside the building, I'm hit with a fresh wave of anxiety. The curtains in the living room are still drawn, the same way I left them. From the outside, it looks untouched. Normal. But I know better. I sit there for a minute, my fingers drumming on the wheel as I scan the street. No unusual cars. No one is loitering. Still, I can't shake the feeling that someone's watching. Waiting.

"Get it together," I mutter to myself before stepping out of the car and locking it behind me. I jog up the steps, my keys already in hand. The door creaks as I push it open, and the smell hits me first—stale air mixed with something faintly metallic. My stomach flips.

The living room is a disaster. Cushions ripped apart, drawers yanked from the coffee table and overturned, their contents strewn across the floor. The recliner, his recliner, is tipped onto its side. My breath catches in my throat. Who the hell did this? The Gardai? Or someone else?

"Shit," I whisper, stepping carefully over the mess. My shoes crunch on broken glass, and I wince, my eyes darting to the source. A photo frame—one of Mark and me from years ago, before everything went to hell. It's been smashed, the photo crumpled and torn. I force myself to look away.

The recliner is empty. No phone. I curse under my breath,

my hands balling into fists. Of course, it's not there. Why would anything go right for once?

I move to the bedroom, stepping over more wreckage. Every drawer has been pulled out and dumped, the mattress flipped onto its side. Whoever did this wasn't just looking—they were sending a message. My pulse quickens as I start rifling through what's left. Socks, shirts, nothing useful. Where is it?

Panic claws at my throat as the minutes slip away. I can't be here too long. Sara's shift ends in less than two hours, and the last thing I need is for her to start asking questions. My fingers shake as I open another drawer, rummaging through the chaos.

That's when I hear it.

A noise. Faint, but distinct. A floorboard creaking just outside the bedroom door.

I freeze, my breath catching in my throat. The air feels suddenly heavier like the walls are closing in. Someone's here.

I grip the edge of the dresser, my heart pounding so hard I can feel it in my ears. My eyes dart to the door, half expecting it to swing open any second. I'm trapped. There's no way out except through the door, and whoever's on the other side…they're not here to help.

My mind races, trying to come up with a plan, but all I can do is stand there, frozen, and pray they don't find me first.

The door creaks open, slow and deliberate. I can't breathe, my chest tightens as if the air's been sucked from the room. But when the figure steps into view, it lunges—and I'm hit with a jolt of relief and dread all at once.

Cian.

87

"What are you doing here?" His voice is a low growl, his sharp eyes taking in the wreckage around us.

"I didn't do that. It was like this." My voice is shaky, defensive.

Cian's gaze flickers back to me, and he nods. "I know."

I blink, caught off guard. "How do you know?"

He steps further into the room, his towering frame filling the small space. Seven feet of muscle and menace, and right now, all of it's directed at me. "Because I did this."

His words hit like a slap, and before I can stop myself, I'm moving toward him. "Did you find a phone?" My voice cracks, desperate. I'm praying he has it. I need it.

Cian's expression doesn't shift as he reaches into his pocket and pulls out the phone. Relief floods me, so overwhelming I almost cry.

"I need it," I say, reaching for it.

He doesn't move, keeping it just out of reach. "Why?"

The weight of his stare is crushing. He's not going to hand it over without an explanation, and for a split second, I consider lying again. But there's no point. Not with him.

"I want to ring Richard," I admit, my voice barely above a whisper. "See if I can sort all this out."

The laugh that escapes Cian's lips is cold, humorless. It sends a shiver down my spine. "Sort it out?" he repeats, his tone mocking. "You think it's that simple?"

"I have to try." My cheeks blaze at his laugh.

"No, you don't. Come on, let's get you home." Cian pockets the phone like that's the end of the conversation.

I shake my head. "I need to do this, Cian," I demand.

"Why? I can sort this out, and I told you not to leave the house."

"Because I couldn't live with myself if something happened to you," I say instead. "Even if you hate me for leaving the house, I needed to try."

His expression softens, just a fraction. "I don't hate you, Luna."

"You should," I whisper, the weight of my past crashing over me. "I'm dragging you into something you didn't ask for."

He steps closer, his voice steady. "You didn't drag me into anything. I'm the one who chose to walk across the road and end his life."

My breath catches. His words hang between us, heavy with unspoken truths. And for the first time, I let myself wonder if maybe, this isn't all my fault.

I glance at Cian, his eyes sharp and unreadable as he watches me. "I could at least try to call Richard," I say, my voice hesitant. "What if he listens to me?"

Cian takes one step closer, closing the already minimal space between us. His presence feels heavier now, more commanding. "Do you really believe that?"

I open my mouth to respond, but the words catch in my throat. Do I believe it? No, not really. But what other options do I have? I swallow hard, my voice barely above a whisper. "I don't, but…I haven't given up yet."

His jaw tightens, but he doesn't argue. "I promise this will all be over soon," he says, his tone gentler than I expected. "But right now, we need to get back to the house."

I want to argue—my mind runs over half a dozen rebuttals, excuses, or ways to stall—but I know better. Cian isn't the type to bend to reasoning, especially when he thinks he's right. "Fine," I say, exhaling through my nose. "I'll follow behind you. I've got Sara's car."

Cian shakes his head firmly, his voice leaving no room for negotiation. "No. You're coming with me. One of my men will bring the car back."

I nod, biting the inside of my cheek to keep from arguing. It's not worth it. The sooner we're out of here, the better. I'm about to step past him when his hand catches my arm, his grip firm but not harsh. The unexpected touch stops me in my tracks.

I look up, and for a moment, I'm caught in the depths of his gaze. There's something there, something intense, but not threatening. His fingers loosen slightly, his thumb brushing my arm. "The day in the bathroom," he says softly, his voice dropping low. "When you walked in on me... I saw something in you. Something so soft and vulnerable."

I freeze, my pulse jumping at his words. He lifts his hand, his rough fingers grazing my cheek, and the gentleness in the gesture catches me off guard. "I knew then that I wanted you, Luna," he murmurs, his tone raw and unapologetic. "And I'll do anything to protect you."

His words cut through me, breaking past the walls I've spent years building. My throat tightens, and I force myself to breathe. "No one's ever tried to protect me before," I admit, my voice barely audible. "Not even my parents."

He nods like he already knows—like he's carried pieces of my story without me having to tell him. There's no pity in his expression, just understanding, and something else I can't quite place. When he leans forward and presses a soft kiss to my forehead, I feel something crack inside me, something I didn't even realize was still whole.

"Then let me protect you," he whispers, his voice a plea, but there's an edge of command in it too. A promise.

I rise up on the tips of my toes, closing the small gap between us, but even then, Cian has to bend down slightly to meet me. My lips brush his, tentative at first, until I feel the warmth of him grounding me.

"Okay," I whisper against his mouth. My hands grip the fabric of his shirt, holding on like it's the only thing keeping me upright. "Please protect me."

CHAPTER ELEVEN

O'REAGAN
AN CHLANN

Luna

The car ride back is silent, except for the hum of the engine and the soft rain tapping against the windshield. I watch Cian out of the corner of my eye, the sharp line of his jaw tight, his hands gripping the steering wheel like it owes him something. His silence feels heavy, loaded with words he won't say yet.

I don't push. I don't dare.

Instead, I stare at the blur of trees and street lights whipping past, their shapes stretching like ghosts. A pit settles in my stomach, the kind that tells me something is coming—something I won't like.

We pull up to the house, and the tension only gets worse. There's another car already here, parked at an odd angle like someone couldn't be bothered to straighten it out. Cian swears under his breath and kills the engine.

"Stay close to me," he says, his voice low and edged with something dark.

I nod, though my heart hammers as I step out into the night. The rain is heavier now, dampening my hair and soaking into my shoes, but I barely notice. The front door swings open before we even get there, and Jack—Cian's cousin—fills the doorway.

"What the fuck took you so long?" Jack growls, his sharp eyes narrowing on us. He's tall and broad, but his presence feels larger than life like he could crush someone with his stare alone. His clothes are rumpled, his face set in a scowl that makes my stomach twist. Something's wrong.

"What happened?" Cian bites out, as Jack backs into the house letting us get out of the rain. Cian's shoulders are squared, his whole body coiled like he's ready for a fight.

Jack runs a hand through his hair, frustration rolling off him in waves. "Richard tried to clip Niall."

The words slam into me like a physical blow. Cian stiffens. I can *feel* the anger radiating off him, sharp and dangerous.

"Is he—?"

"He's fine," Jack says quickly, holding up a hand. "It was close, but he's fine. For now."

Cian exhales, a sound that's part relief, part rage. I take an instinctive step closer to him, the warmth of his arm a small comfort in this sudden, chaotic storm.

Jack doesn't miss it. He shifts his attention to me, and the look he gives me makes my throat tighten. Like I'm the root of the problem, and he knows it. His eyes are the most unusual blue that seems to sear right through my flesh.

"We don't need this shit right now," Jack continues, his tone sharp. "The shipments are coming in, and we're up to our necks already. A turf war? That's the last fucking thing we need."

"Then I'll handle it," Cian growls, the muscles in his jaw flexing.

Jack scoffs, the sound full of disbelief. "Handle it? You think this is *just* your fight? You know better than that, Cian. We're all in this together. You don't get to play hero."

He looks at me again, and this time there's no mistaking the accusation in his eyes. "Richard wants her. You *know* that, don't you? And this ends if—"

"That's not happening." Cian cuts him off, stepping in front of me like a shield. His voice is low and lethal, a tone I've never heard before.

I glance at the back of his head, then at Jack, whose mouth presses into a thin line.

"You're thinking with your heart instead of your head," Jack mutters, his frustration simmering just below the surface. He turns slightly, speaking to both of us now. "We can't keep sitting around waiting to be picked off. We need a plan. A meeting. Tonight."

Cian doesn't argue. "Fine. Call it."

Jack doesn't wait for more. He storms outside, muttering under his breath. The front door slams behind him, leaving me and Cian alone in the hallway. I shiver, but not from the cold.

Cian turns to me, his expression softer now, though his eyes are still dark. Haunted.

"Are you okay?" he asks quietly.

I want to say yes, but the words stick in my throat. How

95

could I be okay? *Niall could've died.* Richard wants *me*. This is my fault. The reality of it crashes over me, and I stagger back a step, sucking in a shaky breath.

Cian reaches for me, his hands firm on my arms. "Hey. Look at me."

I do, though it's hard. His gaze pierces straight through me, searching for something I'm not sure I can give. Reassurance? Hope?

"You're safe here," he says. "I'm not letting him touch you."

I believe him—and that terrifies me more than anything. Because I know what it will cost him to keep that promise. Cian will fight for me. He will bleed for me. He could *die* for me.

And I can't let that happen.

I love the man standing in front of me, with his stormy eyes, scarred knuckles and the unwavering way he protects me like I'm worth something. But love isn't enough to save him.

I have to save him.

Without warning, Cian pulls me into a hug. I sink into his arms, inhaling his scent—a mix of rain, leather, and something uniquely him. I breathe it in like I can memorize it, as if that alone can keep me safe.

No one has ever defended me before. People take. They *take*, and they leave me empty. But not Cian. He's here, and he's real.

This is my chance to give back—to protect someone who sees me completely.

The words *I love you* lodge in my throat, tangled there. Would he laugh if I said them? It feels too fast, too soon…and yet it's so clear.

I want Thursday visits to his nan. I want his lips pressed to mine. I want to learn what makes him the man he is. I want to watch him cook me breakfast or just sit beside him in his car, the silence filling all the cracks I didn't know were there. It's the small things that twist me up inside.

Cian's lips press to mine, soft and searching. A groan slips out before I can stop it.

He deepens the kiss, his hands sliding to my waist and pulling me closer. I melt under his touch, my heart pounding like it might burst through my ribs. The world narrows to just this—his warmth, his lips, the way he tastes like rain, and something darkly sweet. It's the kind of kiss that steals breath and reason, leaving me dizzy and wanting more.

But the moment shatters when we hear someone clearing their throat behind us.

"Cian," a deep voice says. I jerk back, cheeks flushed, as one of his security guys stands at the edge of the door. "Your father's on the office phone."

Cian curses softly, brushing his thumb over my cheek before stepping away. "I'll be back."

I nod, though it feels like something inside me just cracked open.

He disappears into his office, and I'm left standing there, soaked and cold, my lips still tingling.

I can't stay.

The decision hits me like a slap. I know what I have to do.

I climb the stairs slowly, each step feeling heavier than the last. When I reach the room—the one I've been sleeping in—I push the door open and let out a breath I didn't realize I was holding. The space is ridiculous, far too luxurious for someone like me. A four-poster bed sits in the center, its dark wood polished to perfection and the fabric draped around it whispering of wealth and comfort.

I don't linger long. I strip down quickly and step into the shower. The water is scalding hot, almost too hot, but I don't turn it down. It's grounding—a sharp reminder that I'm still here, that this moment is real. My fingers trail through my wet hair, and for a second, I let myself imagine this life is mine: clean, fresh clothes; a bed big enough to get lost in; walls that don't threaten to close in on me.

But that thought barely lasts. My comfort is short-lived, slipping through my fingers like the water swirling down the drain. I'm not stupid. None of this belongs to me.

Once I'm dressed in a set of clothes that are—unsurprisingly—brand new, I pause. I take a minute to really look at the room. The furniture is all polished oak, heavy, and timeless. The curtains are a thick burgundy, and spill onto the floors in elegant folds. Even the air smells different here—clean, expensive, like linen and faint cologne.

I don't belong here.

The realization sits like a weight on my chest. I force myself to breathe through it, to ignore the ache growing in my throat. I should feel grateful—and I do—but all it does is make me more aware of how fleeting this is.

But…I met Cian. And for the first time, I think I understand what it means for someone to protect me. I've never had that before. Not really. And now that I do, it's almost too much. The room feels suffocating. The silence is too loud, pressing against my ears. I need to move.

I slip downstairs to the living room and grab the first book I see from the shelf. It's heavy in my hands, the spine creaking as I open it to a random page. Not that it matters—I don't intend to read it. I just need something to do, something to occupy my hands while my mind refuses to settle.

That's where Cian finds me.

The sound of footsteps makes my head snap up, and there he is, standing in the doorway. For a moment, he doesn't say anything. He just looks at me like he's taking in every detail. Then he crosses the room, his movements slow and deliberate.

He kneels in front of me, his strong hands finding mine, wrapping around them gently. His touch is warm, steady— reassuring in a way I've never experienced before. I hate how much I lean into it.

"I promise this will be over soon," he says quietly. His voice is soft, as if he's trying not to break me with the words. "When I get back, why don't I cook you something nice?"

My throat tightens instantly. I try to swallow it down, but it's no use. He doesn't know. He doesn't understand that I won't be here when he gets back—that I can't be here. I'm leaving, and there's no stopping it.

I want to tell him; to warn him not to get too comfortable. But when I look at his face, at the way he's trying so hard to make this okay for me, the words die on my tongue.

Instead, I force a smile, my lips trembling as I nod. "That sounds nice."

Cian hesitates. I can see it in the way his jaw tightens, the muscles there ticking like he's holding something back. His eyes search my face, and for a second, I think he knows—that he can see right through me. But whatever war he's fighting with himself, he doesn't let it show. Finally, he stands, his hands slipping from mine.

"I won't be long," he says, his voice a little rougher now.

He leaves without another word. I hear the front door open and shut, the soft sound of the engine starting, the tires rolling down the long gravel drive. I sit there, frozen, clutching the book tighter than I need to.

I don't move. Not at first. I tell myself to wait—just a little longer—but the longer I sit, the heavier the silence grows. Finally, I stand, the book slipping from my fingers and thudding against the floor.

Inside the garage, I find a set of keys hanging by the door. My fingers hesitate on the cold metal, the weight somehow heavier than it should be.

The garage is dark except for the faint glow of a single overhead bulb, flickering as though warning me to stop. Three cars sit in the cavernous space, gleaming under the dim light: asensible sedan, a rugged SUV, and then…the sleek black BMW. Its polished surface reflects the pale light, looking both beautiful and dangerous.

I'm sorry, Cian.

The apology tears through my mind as I slide into the driver's seat. I grip the wheel, my hands trembling, slick with sweat. The car hums to life with a low growl, the engine purring like it knows what's coming. For a second, I sit there, my breath shallow and quick, watching the garage door rise inch by inch. The rain outside is relentless, slamming against the concrete drive like a warning— turn back. But I don't. I can't.

As I pull out into the rain-soaked night, the wheels skid briefly on the slick pavement. My heart jumps into my throat, but I press the gas, forcing the car forward. The sound of the rain drowns out everything—the roar of the engine, the sound of my breaths, even the voice screaming at me in the back of my head to stop.

I know where Richard lives. I know what I'm walking into.

The drive is a blur of headlights, rain streaks, and wipers squealing against the glass. My knuckles turn white against the wheel. Every turn, every shadow feels like it's watching me, closing in. I try to focus on the road, but my mind won't stop spinning.

By the time I pull up to Richard's sprawling house, my heart feels like it might explode. The mansion looms ahead, a dark silhouette against the stormy sky. Every window glows faintly, casting eerie light through the sheets of rain. My chest tightens as I see them—two men already waiting by the front drive. Their silhouettes are sharp, unmoving, like statues carved out of the night itself.

I slow the car, and they move. My stomach twists violently as they step forward, boots splashing through puddles. Before I've even stopped fully, they're there—one on each side. Rainwater drips from their faces, but they don't flinch. Their hands rest on their weapons. Ready.

One of them raps on the window hard enough to make me jump.

I slowly roll it down, letting rain find its way into the car. "Richard is expecting me; tell him Luna is here."

One of the men has his hand resting on his gun while the other speaks into a walkie-talkie; I'm sure he's letting Richard know I'm here. After a moment, the man turns back to me.

"Get out," one growls, his voice a low rumble that cuts through the storm.

I do as they say, every movement slow, deliberate, as though I can fool them into thinking I'm not terrified. The rain soaks through my clothes instantly, cold and punishing. My knees threaten to give out, but I lift my chin and step out, pretending I'm stronger than I feel.

The taller man keeps his gaze fixed on me, his eyes like stone, unblinking. His partner's fingers twitch near the holster of his gun. They're waiting for something—a signal, maybe, or just one wrong move. The silence is broken by a crackle, sharp and jarring, from the walkie-talkie clipped to the taller man's belt.

Richard's voice bursts through the static, cold and unmistakable.

"Bring her to me."

This is it.

One of them grips my arm, not painfully, but firmly enough to remind me that I'm not going anywhere. They guide me forward, and with every step toward the house, my pulse pounds harder. The massive doors are waiting, cracked open just enough to show a sliver of light inside. My heart screams at me to run, but my legs keep moving.

The doors close behind us with a deafening thud, and suddenly, the storm outside feels mild compared to what's brewing inside this house.

CHAPTER TWELVE

O'REAGAN
AN CHLANN

Cian

The table is crowded, a rare occurrence when we're all in the same room—Jack, my cousin, and Liam's son; my uncles Finn and Darragh; and my father. The air is thick with tension, the kind that wraps around you and refuses to let go, the kind only men who live in shadows understand. The heavy wood table between us feels more like a battlefield than a gathering place, and every glance exchanged carries the weight of unspoken histories.

Liam stands at the head of the table, commanding the space with his presence alone. His sharp gaze sweeps over us like a general appraising his troops, his words measured and cold, each one landing with precision.

"We've got the locations," Liam begins, his voice as steady as a sniper's aim. "Our inside man confirmed their strongholds. We hit them all in one night, take them out before they even know what's happening. Five locations."

The words settle over the room like a shroud. My father leans back in his chair, arms crossed, his expression unreadable, but his eyes burn with the quiet ferocity of a man who's been through too many battles to count. Finn shifts uneasily. Killing's never sat well with him, no matter how necessary it becomes. Across from him, Darragh is his mirror opposite—relaxed, almost amused. His smirk is a weapon in itself, and his fingers drum out a casual rhythm on the table as though this were a game he'd already won. An unlit cigarette sits behind his left ear; no doubt it will be lit the minute we vacate the room.

Jack sits to my left, his posture as calm and calculated as his father's. His eyes flick around the room, measuring everyone. He's Liam's son through and through—destined to lead us one day, whether he wants the mantle or not.

"What's the order?" Finn asks, his voice smooth, almost bored, but the tension in his jaw betrays him. He knows what's coming, and so do I.

Liam's response is swift and clinical. He pulls a map from his jacket, spreading it out on the table with a flick of his wrist. The creases catch the dim overhead light, throwing shadows across the bold red marks that signal our targets.

"We split into teams," he says, tapping the first four locations with the tip of a pen. "These are smaller, less guarded. Quick work. The fifth…" His finger lands on the final mark, pressing it down as though he could crush it beneath his touch. "Richard's house. It's fortified, heavily guarded. But by the time we hit it, they'll already be scrambling from the chaos of the first four strikes. That's when we move."

The room falls silent. Even the rhythm of Darragh's fingers halts.

"And the inside man?" My voice cuts through the quiet, the question sharp and deliberate. I lean forward, meeting Liam's gaze head-on.

For a moment, the only sound is the faint hum of the overhead light. Liam's eyes lock onto mine, colder than I've ever seen them, and when he speaks, it's with a calm that sends a chill through the room.

"He wants to walk away."

Darragh snorts, a low, derisive laugh that grates against the tension already coiled tight in my chest. "And you'll let him?" His tone is mocking, but there's an edge of curiosity there, a challenge veiled in his amusement.

Liam shakes his head slowly; his one word is calculated and cruel. "No."

The word hangs in the air like a death sentence. For a heartbeat, no one speaks. No one moves. This is who Liam is—controlled, relentless, and utterly without mercy. It's why he leads us. It's why we follow him.

"I'll take Richard's house," Liam continues, his voice cutting through the silence like a blade. "I've got ex-military coming in for the job. It'll be clean, precise. No room for mistakes."

The rest of us nod, but the weight of what's coming settles over me like a second skin. The plan is set, the lines drawn. And like all games in our world, it ends in blood.

The meeting wraps up quickly after that. Assignments are handed out with precision, each of us knowing exactly what's at stake. One by one, we leave.

Outside, the flick of a lighter pierces the silence as Darragh leans against the wall, igniting his cigarette with practiced ease. A thin wisp of smoke curls into the twilight, its scent sharp and acrid. Finn lingers beside him, his posture stiff, shoulders tense.

I don't linger. The weight in my chest demands motion, so I shove my hands deep into my pockets and make my way to my car, each step heavy with the mental replay of the plan. Every detail races through my mind, every contingency scrutinized. It has to work. It *must* work. We don't have another choice.

When I arrive home, the first sign that something's off hits me like a slap to the face. The garage door hums open, revealing the glaring absence of one of my cars. An empty space that shouldn't be empty where my new BMW had been parked.

A sinking feeling coils in my gut, ice-cold and nauseating. Luna.

I rush inside, pulling my phone from my pocket with shaking hands. My fingers swipe the screen with practiced precision, opening the tracker app linked to my vehicles. My breath catches when the screen lights up with a location.

Richard's house.

My stomach drops, a hollow, lurching sensation that leaves me gripping the edge of the counter for support. A storm brews in my chest, rage and fear battling for dominance.

I hit the call button for Liam. One ring. Two. It goes to voicemail.

"Dammit!" I hiss, pacing the length of the kitchen as I try again. Same result.

I race upstairs, but I know she isn't here. The empty room confirms my suspicions.

Next, I call my father. Surely, he'll answer. He always does.

But the line rings out, and the silence on the other end only fans the flames of my growing panic.

"For fuck's sake!" My voice echoes off the walls, sharp and desperate.

I scroll through my contacts, landing on the last name I want to see. Jack. But at this moment, I don't have the luxury of choice. I grit my teeth and press the call button, my jaw tightening as the phone rings.

When he picks up, his voice is as infuriatingly casual as ever.

"What?" Jack snaps, his tone clipped and already laced with impatience.

"Luna," I bite out, pacing the room like a caged animal. "She's at Richard's. One of my cars is gone."

There's a pause, long enough to hear my own pulse pounding in my ears. Then Jack growls, low and sharp, "She's handing herself over."

The words hit like a fist to the gut. My body moves on instinct, grabbing my keys off the counter. "We need to get her. Now."

"Okay," Jack mutters. In the background, I hear the rustle of movement—he's already preparing. "I'll come with you and bring backup."

I don't waste time arguing. Jack's irritating, but he's not wrong.

When I pull up to his place which is close to my house, he's waiting outside, leaning against a black duffel bag slung over his shoulder. His expression is set in stone, eyes narrowed, and jaw clenched. He tosses the bag into the backseat and climbs in beside me, his movements sharp, controlled.

"She's a liability," Jack says as I hit the gas. "You should've seen this coming."

"I knew something was off," I admit, gripping the wheel until my knuckles ache. "But this… this is something else." Yet, I think of how my father and Jack had mentioned handing her over in front of her; I wonder if that was the deciding factor for her. She's too kind and doesn't seem to see the value in herself. But, I see it.

Jack doesn't respond immediately; instead, pulls out his phone and punches in a number. When no one picks up, he curses under his breath and leaves a voice message for my father.

"We're going to Richard's now. Luna is inside; we will pull her out before you make the hit, but wait for us to leave."

The way he says *we*, sends a chill down my spine. Jack's voice is cold, calculated—a far cry from the usual sharp-edged arrogance he wears like armor. He's serious now, and that makes him dangerous. For the first time tonight, I wonder if bringing him along was a mistake. We don't get along even during the best of times, but I had no one else to call.

Backup cars follow in our wake, their headlights cutting through the darkness like watchful eyes. It should bring some comfort, but it doesn't. The weight in my chest only grows heavier as we close the distance to Richard's estate.

I can't shake the image of Luna walking into the lion's den, her head held high, defiance burning in her eyes. Whatever her reasons, whatever plan she's concocted in her reckless, brilliant mind, doesn't matter anymore.

She's mine to protect. Always will be.

And I'll be damned if I let her slip away tonight.

As we near Richard's estate, I slowly pull over; I don't want them to know we are coming.

"We get her out, and we don't linger. No heroics, leave the cleanup to my dad," Jack says.

I glance at him, his face illuminated by the pale glow of the dashboard lights. There's no humor there, no trace of his usual bravado.

"Whatever it takes," I say, my voice a quiet promise.

Jack nods, his jaw tightening. "Just try and stick to the plan." We get out, and Jack removes several guns from his duffel bag, loading his body with them before he hands me two. Once we are all set, we go on foot; all the other cars have pulled in behind us, and the men slowly get out, everyone checking their weapons. They don't look to me for orders but to Jack.

" Cian and I will go in first. I need you all to be ready if you hear gunfire or if we don't return."

They all nod in unison.

We move slowly down the road, keeping to the edge of the road.

The estate looms ahead, its silhouette stark against the night sky.

It's time.

The weight of the moment settles over me as we move toward the estate, shadows blending with the darkness. Somewhere inside, Luna is waiting—whether she knows it or not.

And I'll stop at nothing to bring her back.

CHAPTER THIRTEEN

O'REAGAN
AN CHLANN

Cian

The gravel crunches softly beneath Jack's boots as he comes to a halt. His hand moves deliberately, reaching down to pick up a jagged stone. In the same motion, he pulls his gun from its holster, the silencer already screwed on tight. He glances at me, the faint gleam in his eyes catching the moonlight. I know that look. It's a silent question, and my answer is always the same.

I nod, the weight of my weapon a comforting reminder in my hand. Carefully, I twist the silencer into place, keeping my movements precise and silent. Jack's fingers twitch, and he launches the stone into the air with practiced ease. It arcs high, disappearing for a moment before clattering noisily against the roof of the security outhouse.

The response is immediate. Inside, we hear the muffled sound of boots scraping on concrete. Voices—three, maybe four. The gates groan on their hinges as they start to open, just enough for one man to step out and scan the area. He's cautious, staying close to the shadow of the wall. A tactical move, smart, but not smart enough.

Jack holds his position, his finger flexing slightly against the trigger. I stay crouched in the darkness beside him, every muscle tense. The guard doesn't take the bait, doesn't step far enough away for us to strike without exposing ourselves. My chest tightens. Jack's plan is slipping through our fingers.

Then he picks up another stone.

I exhale slowly, forcing myself to stay calm as he lobs it farther this time, the sharp sound echoing off the walls. The guard reacts instantly, pulling his weapon and stepping to the side of the road. His gaze pierces the darkness, scanning for threats he can't see.

That's when Jack fires. The silenced shot is barely a whisper, but it's deafening to me. The guard crumples where he stands, a single shot to the head sending him sprawling on the ground. Blood pools beneath him, dark and glistening in the faint light. So much for getting in and out clean.

I move with Jack, both of us inching closer to the gate, the tension between us electric. A second man appears in the gateway, his gun drawn. Before he has time to process what's happened, I line up my shot and pull the trigger. He drops silently, his body slumping back into the shadows.

It's too easy. Too quiet. My instincts scream at me just as the third man emerges, but he doesn't come out into the open like the others. He's smarter, holding back just enough to stay in cover. My heart pounds in my chest as I try to calculate the odds, but then the unmistakable sound of gears grinding fills the air.

"The gates," I hiss under my breath. They're closing.

Jack doesn't respond. He's already moving, his posture low and his weapon raised. There's no time to think, no time to plan. I'm right behind him, every nerve in my body on fire as we close the distance between us and the rapidly shrinking gap. One wrong move, one hesitation, and we'll be locked out—or worse, pinned down with no entry.

I can feel the weight of the night pressing in on us, heavy and suffocating. The third man is still out there, somewhere in the shadows, and I know he's waiting. Waiting for us to make a mistake.

"Move," Jack says. I do. "Take out the cameras," Jack orders, and I focus on the cameras on either side of the gate, taking them out one by one with quick, precise shots. The third man fires at Jack but misses. Jack doesn't. His return shot finds its mark, and the man collapses in a heap just as the gates are nearly closed. Jack moves fast, grabbing the nearest dead body and wedging it between the gates, halting their progress.

"Go," he growls. We still have to shift sideways to squeeze through the narrow gap, every movement tight and deliberate. Inside, the radio on the waistband of one of the fallen guards crackles to life, the sound like a jolt to my nerves.

"Everything okay down at the gates?"

The voice is calm, but we know better. We're out of time.

Jack and I move up the long driveway, sticking close to the hedge line. The night air is still, but my pulse pounds like a war drum in my ears. Every step is deliberate, each one calculated to avoid the crunch of gravel. The house looms ahead, its darkened windows glinting faintly under the pale moonlight. It looks quiet, but we both know better.

A faint buzz catches my ear—mechanical and subtle. I freeze, my eyes scanning until I spot it: a sleek black camera mounted above the garage. Its lens sweeps the area, a tiny red light blinking with the rhythm of a heartbeat. I raise my pistol, steady my breathing, and pull the trigger. The silencer muffles the shot, but the sparks that erupt from the camera's shattered body are bright in the darkness. It droops lifelessly against its mount.

Jack nods approvingly, and we press forward. We're halfway to the house when the front door creaks open, spilling a faint beam of warm light onto the stone steps. Two men step outside, their postures casual, unaware of the danger creeping closer. They're talking in low voices, but their words are lost because of the distance. One of them pauses mid-sentence, his foot crunching on the shards of the destroyed camera. He glances down, then up, his eyes narrowing in alarm.

He doesn't get the chance to shout. Jack emerges from the hedge line like a ghost, his movements fluid and silent. The pistol in his hand barks twice, the suppressed shots blending into the night. Both men collapse, one crumpling against the doorframe, the other spilling onto the path—the warm light pools around their still forms.

"Door's open," Jack mutters, his voice barely audible. His eyes scan the area, sharp and vigilant.

I nod, my own gaze sweeping the property for any additional cameras. None. That's good—if we can blind the men inside, this becomes a different game—a winnable one.

We approach the house slowly, the faint scent of fresh-cut grass mingling with the metallic tang of blood in the air. Jack reaches the door first, his back pressed against the frame as he peeks inside. He glances at me, a quick nod signaling the all-clear.

I step through the doorway, my gun held steady in front of me. The house's interior is a stark contrast to the tense darkness outside. Soft classical music drifts through the air, its elegant notes weaving a strange, haunting melody. It's coming from somewhere deeper within the house, but the echo makes it hard to pinpoint.

The entryway is grand—marble floors, an ornate chandelier hanging overhead. I scan the room, my grip tightening on my weapon.

"Clear," I whisper over my shoulder to Jack, who slips in behind me. His presence is a solid reassurance, even though we're walking into the lion's den.

A movement catches my eye—just a flicker at the edge of my vision. I turn quickly, training my gun on a hallway that branches off to the right. Nothing. Just shadows playing tricks.

"They know we're here," Jack says quietly. His voice is low, calm, but I hear the edge in it. He's right. The men in this house don't need cameras to sense a threat. They've survived this long for a reason.

I nod, swallowing hard, and press forward.

Each room we pass is lifeless, the silence only broken by the faint hum of distant music growing louder. My pulse hammers in my ears, anticipation and dread warring inside me. The source is close now.

Jack walks beside me, his movements fluid but deliberate.

Finally, we reach the end of the corridor. The door ahead is slightly ajar, and from my angle, I catch sight of the back of someone's head. It's drooped forward, their body slumped unnaturally. My breath catches, chest tightening painfully.

Luna.

Without thinking, I step forward, my hand reaching for the handle. But before I can grip it, Jack's strong hand clamps over mine. I whip my head toward him, eyes narrowing, but the look on his face stops me cold. His lips are pressed into a grim line, his dark eyes hard as stone. He gives a subtle shake of his head. He doesn't need to speak for me to understand. This is a trap.

But I can't stand here and do nothing. I glance back through the crack in the door. Luna stirs, a faint groan escaping her lips. Relief and rage collide within me, almost knocking me off balance. She's alive. But she's bound to a chair, her arms restrained tightly behind her back.

That's when I hear it—the distinct, gut-wrenching click of a gun being cocked behind me.

"You got further than I thought you would," a voice drawls, smooth and smug.

My body goes rigid, the adrenaline spiking through my veins as I turn slowly to face him. Richard stands there, flanked by a small army of men, all with their guns trained on Jack and me. His smile is a cruel slash across his face, one that makes my stomach churn.

"Drop your weapons," Richard orders, his tone laced with mockery, as though he's already won.

I let a smirk curl my lips, refusing to let him see how the odds are stacking against us. "Just give me Luna, and I'll let you all live." My voice is calm and confident.

Richard laughs, a low, guttural sound that grates against my nerves. "I don't think you're seeing the situation clearly, friend. There are eight guns pointed at your head. You're outnumbered, outgunned, and out of options."

"Oh, I see just fine," I say smoothly, tilting my head. "But you don't really think we came alone, do you? That would be foolish."

The smirk slips from Richard's face, replaced by a flicker of uncertainty. He glances sharply at three of his men. "Check the perimeter," he snaps.

As they move to obey, I do a quick mental calculation. That leaves five of them in the room. Five against us? Doable, but not without risk. My mind races for a plan, my hand tightening on my weapon.

"Drop your weapons," Richard repeats, his voice sharper now, more insistent.

Jack moves first, his jaw clenched so tightly I can almost hear his teeth grinding. He lowers his gun to the ground with deliberate slowness, then kicks it over to Richard with more force than necessary. The heavy clang echoes in the charged silence. Richard's gaze snaps back to me, expectant.

Reluctantly, I follow suit, dropping my gun and sending it skidding across the floor. The moment it leaves my hand, two of Richard's men close in on me, their intentions clear.

But they've underestimated us.

Jack strikes first, a blur of motion, as he lunges at the closest man. He wrests the gun from the guy's grip and uses him as a human shield, firing over his shoulder with ruthless precision. The room erupts into chaos, bullets flying and men shouting. I dive for cover, adrenaline sharpening my every move.

Jack ducks into a side room, dragging me with him as we

regroup. He fires several quick shots through the window, the glass shattering with a deafening crash. It's enough to send a message to our men outside. They wouldn't have heard our earlier shots because we used silencers, but the last few bangs are loud enough to wake the dead.

Then, just as planned, reinforcements arrive. Gunfire explodes in the hallway, a cacophony of controlled chaos. I catch a glimpse of our men charging in, their movements practiced and efficient. The tide is turning.

But it's not over yet.

Jack and I re-enter the fray, taking advantage of the distraction to eliminate two more of Richard's men. I fight my way toward Luna, my focus narrowing to a single point: her.

Richard retreats, but not before locking eyes with me, his expression a promise of vengeance. I don't care. He can't run far enough.

Finally, I reach her, my hands working quickly to untie the ropes that bite into her wrists. She's dazed, her head lolling slightly, but when her eyes meet mine, there's recognition. Relief floods through me, almost buckling my knees.

"I've got you," I murmur, my voice low but fierce. "You're safe now."

The fight rages on around us, but for a moment, it's just the two of us. And that's enough to keep me going.

I almost have Luna out of the chair. Her head lolls against my chest, her eyes fluttering but unfocused. She's unharmed—at least, I don't see any visible injuries—but it's clear she's been drugged. Her body is limp, unable to hold itself up, and I tighten my arm around her waist to keep her from collapsing.

"It's okay," I murmur, more for my own reassurance than hers. "I've got you."

She doesn't respond, just lets out a faint sigh as I help her rise. The weight of her against me fuels my determination to get her out of here, away from this nightmare.

Then I see him.

A man appears in the doorway, his gun raised, the barrel aimed directly at Luna. My breath catches, my body tensing as I realize I won't have time to reach my own gun. *Damn it.* Without thinking, I pivot, putting myself between Luna and the weapon, bracing for the inevitable.

This is it.

The shot rings out.

I wait for the pain, the fire of a bullet tearing through me— but it never comes. Instead, there's a loud thud. I snap my head up, heart hammering, to see the man lying motionless on the floor. Blood pools beneath him, his lifeless eyes staring at nothing.

Standing over him is my father, his gun still in his hand.

He meets my gaze and gives a quick nod. "Get her out of here."

Relief surges through me, but I don't waste time replying. I tighten my grip on Luna, scooping her into my arms. She's so light, too light, and the thought unsettles me more than I care to admit. Her cheek presses against my shoulder, and I feel her warm, shallow breaths against my neck.

"I've got you," I whisper again, more fiercely this time. "You're safe now."

As I step out of the room, chaos greets me—men shouting, the distant echoes of gunfire. But my eyes land on Liam, standing over Richard's body. Blood stains his hands and clothes, but he looks calm, almost eerily so. He glances at me, then at Luna in my arms, and nods once.

"It's done," he says coldly. Then, louder, to the men around us: "Burn it. Everyone, clear out."

The air smells of blood, gunpowder, and death, but I don't care. It's over.

Luna is safe.

CHAPTER FOURTEEN

O'REAGAN
AN CHLANN

Cian

Jack's office is exactly as I remember it—dark, imposing, and suffocatingly expensive. The walls are lined with shelves filled with leather-bound books I doubt he's ever read, and the massive desk between us is made of some glossy wood that probably costs more than my car. Jack sits behind it like a king on his throne, his chair too large, his tailored suit too perfect. He looks up from the papers in front of him, a glass of whiskey in one hand, and fixes me with the same indifferent gaze he always has.

"Cian," he says, leaning back. His voice is smooth, calculated, like he already knows the end of every conversation before it even starts. "To what do I owe the pleasure?"

It's a formality. There's no pleasure in this for either of us.

"I came to thank you," I say, my tone stiff. "For stepping in when you didn't have to."

He raises a brow, the faintest smirk tugging at the corner of his mouth. "Didn't have to?" He swirls the whiskey lazily in his glass, the ice clinking. "Let's not rewrite history, Cian. You needed me, and I delivered. Let's leave it at that."

I grit my teeth. This is why I can't stand him—always so smug, so untouchable. Still, he's right. We needed him, and he came through. Begrudgingly, I nod.

"It's over," I say, more to myself than him. "Three weeks, and the news is still eating it up. Gang war this, gang war that. They blame Richard's own men for killing his son, Mark, and then trying to overthrow Richard, saying it caused an internal collapse."

Jack shrugs, unbothered. "That's what we pay the Gardai for."

I want to argue, to call him out on his arrogance, but what's the point? Jack and I will never see eye to eye. We've tolerated each other out of necessity; our fathers are brothers, that's the only reason we must appear to be getting along. The silence stretches, thick and uncomfortable, until he finally waves me off.

"You've said your piece. Now, if you'll excuse me, I have work to do."

I hesitate, the words lodged in my throat. Finally, I let them spill out. "I know your father keeps a watch over our properties, so I wanted to let you know I've given Luna one of the apartments on Abbey's Creek."

His eyes flicker with amusement, and the corner of his mouth quirks up again. That damn smirk. "They are nice apartments," he says, his tone deceptively casual.

I nod, refusing to rise to the bait.

"Does she know you're her landlord?" he asks, leaning forward slightly, his sneer cutting through me like a blade.

"No. It's best if we keep it between us."

Jack hums, clearly unimpressed, and leans back again, his gaze drifting to the papers on his desk. "You should tell my father. It's not my area." He looks up briefly, just long enough to twist the knife. "I'm over the clubs."

I stiffen, my stomach twisting. "I was hoping you could tell him for me."

His expression doesn't change, but the dismissiveness in his voice is unmistakable. "Sorry, but I'm all out of charity right now." He waves me off again, not even bothering to look up. "Close the door on your way out."

I turn on my heel, biting down on the string of curses that are fighting to escape. The man might be powerful, but he's a bastard through and through. The door clicks shut behind me, and I exhale sharply, dragging a hand through my hair. Now, I have no choice but to speak to Liam, Jack's father. The thought makes my skin crawl. Liam doesn't just trade in power—he collects debts like trophies. Giving Luna that apartment will come at a cost if Liam gets involved, and I'll be the one paying it.

Checking my watch, I realize it's nearly lunchtime. Luna will be at the café—same place, same time, like clockwork. I need to see her. Maybe I still have time.

Sliding into my car parked outside the club, I grip the wheel tighter than I should, my mind racing.

Fuck.

I honestly had thought if I thanked Jack for his help he might just agree to tell his father. I'm sure Liam wouldn't expect anything in return from his son, but I'm not his son.

I pick up the phone, and for the first time, I pray he doesn't answer.

"Cian." Liam's one word makes me clench the phone tighter.

"Hi, Liam. I know you're busy, so I won't keep you long." I start.

"I always have time for my nephew." Liam's drawl is already calculating.

"I've set Luna up in one of the apartments on Abbey's Creek. I spoke to Jack about it and said I'd give you a ring."

"That was wise," he answers.

I'm not sure if that's about giving Luna an apartment or calling him about it.

Liam doesn't expand on what was wise but continues to speak.

"She will have the apartment for as long as she needs." He finishes.

"Thank you." I'm ready to end the call, but Liam isn't.

"I normally wouldn't be so quick to hand over one of our luxury apartments, but for you, Cian, I will write this off."

My free hand tightens on the steering wheel. "Thanks," I mumble.

"I'm sure there will be a way you can repay me."

I knew it; nothing came free with Liam. "Anytime, Liam." I finish.

"Great." He finishes, and the line goes dead. He will call me up on that favor, but it's not today. Today, I get to see Luna.

The small café is a stark contrast to Jack's office—bright, warm, and alive with the soft hum of conversation. I spot Luna immediately, sitting alone at a corner table. She's poking at her salad, lost in

128

thought, her hair falling in soft waves around her face. It's been three weeks since the attack, and she wanted a fresh start, her own place, so that's why I got her one. I just haven't shared with her that I'm her landlord. Not having her under my roof doesn't mean I've let her out of my sight. My men have been watching her, keeping her safe. She doesn't know, and she doesn't need to.

I slide into the seat beside her without warning. She startles, her fork clattering against her plate, but when she sees me, her expression softens into something unreadable.

"Cian," she says, her voice tentative. "What are you doing here?"

I lean back in the chair, watching her closely. She looks better—healthier, stronger—but there's still a shadow in her eyes that wasn't there before.

"I was in the area and spotted you through the window," I say simply.

She tilts her head; humor lights up her hazel eyes. "So, you were just in the area?"

I meet her gaze, holding it. "Yes. How are you settling in?"

She picks up her fork and loads it with greens but doesn't pop the food into her mouth. "I love my apartment; thank you so much again for helping me find it."

I wave off her praise. "Is there anything else you need?"

"How about telling the men who are always following me to leave me alone? I assume they are yours since they only watch me."

I can't stop the soft laugh. "I'm just keeping …."

She cuts me off. "Safe. I know." She reaches across the table and places her hand on me. "I know, Cian. That's why I had to leave. I can't be your responsibility. You have done more for me than anyone in my life."

"You deserve it and so much more," I say and mean it.

Her cheeks heat up.

"I have something to tell you," she says, her eyes light up.

"I took the job at the nursing home."

"That's great news." I can't stop the smile that spreads across my face.

"So, I'll see you every Thursday then?" She pops the food into her mouth.

I can't look away from her lips. "I'm available every day of the week."

She covers her mouth as she laughs softly. I give her a moment to chew and swallow her food.

A waitress arrives, an interference I could do without. "A coffee, please," I say before she even asks so she will fuck off. She nods and runs along.

"You are always welcome." Luna finally says.

"How about tonight?" I can't look away from her lips.

"I'm free. But, my friend Becca might be staying with me for a while."

I nod. "Will she be there tonight?" I pause as the waitress places the coffee in front of me.

"Would you like a refill?" she asks Luna.

Luna places her hand over her mug. "No, thank you."

"I actually think she is working," Luna says, and her cheeks deepen in color.

"I shall see you tonight then." I rise and place a kiss on her forehead before going to the counter.

"I'll pay for table four."

The teller rings up Luna's food, and I pay. On the way out, I know Luna is watching me leave, and when I glance over my shoulder, she gives me one of her rare smiles. That's what I want to spend the rest of my life doing, making her smile.

EPILOGUE

O'REAGAN
AN CHLANN

Luna

The nursing home hums with gentle activity. The soft murmur of conversations, the occasional burst of laughter, and the distant clatter of dishes create a peaceful rhythm. I'm perched on the edge of a chair in the lounge, my cheeks aching from how much I've been smiling.

"You're a natural with them," Mary, one of the nurses, says as she hands me a cup of tea.

"They're the highlight of my week," I admit, taking the cup. The warmth seeps into my hands, and I glance over at Mrs. Callahan, who's telling another exaggerated story about her younger days. The staff and a few residents are laughing heartily, and I can't help but join in.

It feels so good to be here, to feel useful and connected. My heart feels full, and as I say my goodbyes and step into the crisp afternoon air, I realize I'm genuinely happy.

The drive back to my apartment is peaceful. As I park and glance up at my building, a wave of gratitude washes over me.

This place—this perfect little sanctuary—is mine. I still can't believe my luck.

Grabbing the grocery bags from the trunk, I head inside, my steps light, and I ride the elevator up. The familiar ding announces my floor, and as the doors slide open, my breath catches.

Cian is standing there, leaning casually against the wall, his dark hair slightly tousled and his dark brown eyes lighting up when he sees me. My heart skips a beat, then thuds in my chest.

"This is a lovely surprise," I say, unable to keep the smile off my face.

He steps forward and takes the bags from my hands. "This could be a daily occurrence if you want," he teases, his voice low and warm.

I laugh, but I know he's not entirely joking. If I so much as hinted at it, Cian would move in without hesitation or insist I live with him. And while the idea tempts me, I need my space. I need to learn to stand on my own two feet.

"Come on," I say, leading the way to my apartment door.

Inside, I stop short, my eyes landing on the massive bouquet of flowers sitting on the coffee table. The arrangement is stunning, a riot of colors and fragrances that fill the air. I glance back at Cian, but his expression is anything but pleased. His jaw tightens as he sets the groceries down and strides to the flowers, pulling the small white card from among the blooms.

"Who is it from?" I ask, moving closer. His back is rigid, his fingers gripping the card tightly. I catch a glimpse of the name scrawled at the bottom before he can crumple it.

Liam.

"Who's Liam?" I ask, my voice quiet but curious.

He hesitates, his stormy gaze flicking to mine. After a moment, he exhales and hands me the card.

Welcome to the building, Luna. – Liam.

"He's the landlord," Cian says, his voice clipped.

I inhale deeply, letting the scent of the flowers fill my lungs. "That was so lovely of him," I say with a small smile. But when I look back at Cian, his tension hasn't eased. Something about this is bothering him, though I can't quite put my finger on what.

"Is everything okay?" I ask softly.

He shrugs out of his jacket and crosses the space between us, his hands settling gently on my shoulders. He leans down and presses a kiss to my forehead. "Everything is perfect," he murmurs.

And when I look up into his eyes, the worry in his gaze melts away, replaced by something warm and steady. My chest swells, and I can't help but smile. How did I get so lucky to have him in my life?

Cian's gaze softens, but then it shifts into something else—something hungry. He steps closer, his hands sliding to my waist, and before I can say anything, his lips crash into mine. The kiss is demanding, intense, like nothing I've ever experienced. My arms wind around his neck instinctively, and I exhale into his mouth as his tongue tangles with mine, sending a spark straight through me.

His hand tightens at my waist, pulling me against him, and suddenly I'm airborne. He lifts me effortlessly, as if I weigh nothing, and I wrap my legs around his waist, feeling the hard press of his excitement against my stomach. Heat pools low in my belly, and a new kind of want unfurls inside me—raw and overwhelming.

We've never done more than kiss before, but I've never

135

wanted anyone the way I want Cian right now. And from the way his hands roam my back, and his kisses grow more frantic, I know he feels the same.

I tighten my hold on his shoulders, gasping as he breaks the kiss and peppers soft ones along my jaw and down my neck. Each touch of his lips sends shivers down my spine. He turns and strides toward the bedroom, nudging the door open with his foot.

The bed feels soft beneath me as he lowers me onto it, his body hovering over mine. He pauses, his dark brown eyes sweeping over me with an intensity that makes my breath catch. The image of him flashes in my mind—the first day I saw him at work, stepping out of the shower, unabashedly naked. He was... huge. The memory sends a flush to my cheeks, and I bite my lip as I meet his gaze.

Cian's lips curl into a small, knowing smile. "You're beautiful," he whispers, his voice rough with need.

My heart pounds, and I reach up, brushing my fingers along his jaw. "So are you," I whisper back, and then he's kissing me again.

His kisses grow even more frantic, his lips moving as if he's trying to devour me. My fingers fumble at the buttons of his shirt, trembling with anticipation and the need to feel his skin against mine. "Take off your clothes," I whisper into his mouth, my voice a mix of desperation and excitement.

He pulls back instantly, his breathing ragged, and then he's off me, peeling off his clothes with a speed that leaves me breathless. I barely have time to tug my trousers down before he's standing naked in front of me. My breath catches at the sight of him, his body taut and powerful, every line of him exuding raw masculinity.

He steps between my legs, his presence overwhelming, and leans down to slowly unbutton my uniform top. His fingers move with an agonizing slowness, each button undone with deliberate care. The anticipation is almost painful, and a heat pools between my legs, leaving me aching for his touch.

As he works, his dark eyes stay locked on mine, a silent promise passing between us. I've never felt so exposed, so wanted, and as he slides the fabric from my shoulders, I close my eyes and allow my body to soak up every single touch.

Cian's hands trail down, his touch igniting every nerve as he moves across my breasts, which seem to swell under his fingers. His hands glide over my stomach, slow and deliberate, before reaching my thighs. He pushes them apart, his movements commanding, giving himself access to me.

My breath hitches, my eyes shooting open as he positions himself. I feel the head of him press against my entrance, the sensation sending a shiver up my spine. He pushes in slowly, the stretch stealing my breath as he begins to fill me. My body reacts, expanding to accommodate him, the pressure unlike anything I've felt before.

He pulls back, sliding almost out, only to push in again, each movement deliberate. I can tell he's holding back, his control clear on his face as he leans over me, his hands planted firmly on either side of my head. His gaze meets mine, and the intensity in his eyes sends a wave of heat crashing over me.

Wrapping my legs around his waist, I press my heels into him, urging him closer, deeper. My fingers dig into his shoulders, anchoring myself to him as my body adjusts to his size, the pleasure building with every movement. Cian groans, the sound low and guttural, and it sends a thrill through me, my heart pounding in time with each thrust.

I know he's filled me completely; the sensation is overwhelming. It's all-consuming, like fire dancing across my skin—dangerous, yet it doesn't burn. Cian moves faster, harder, and I cry out with each thrust, my voice rising uncontrollably.

A large hand grips my chin, tilting my face up, and I meet his dark, intense gaze. His eyes burn with a feral hunger as he fucks me hard, each powerful stroke pushing me to my limits. The intensity sends my vocal cords straining to a pitch I didn't know I was capable of.

The build in my stomach grows, a wave rolling across my skin, tightening every muscle in its path. My fingers grip his forearms, desperate for an anchor as he drives into me with an unrelenting force I've never experienced. My entire body is coiled, trembling on the edge, until the wave crests.

I scream as my orgasm tears through me, a hurricane of sensation that leaves me shaking, utterly consumed. Cian's movements don't falter, and the aftershocks ripple through me, leaving me breathless and completely undone in his arms. He continues his relentless pounding, his rhythm never faltering until he cries out, his own release tearing through him. His body shudders as he lowers himself onto me, his weight grounding me as our mingled breaths fill the quiet room. The intensity ebbs, leaving only the sound of our shared exhaustion and the steady thrum of our heartbeats.

Lying in Cian's arms, I feel a warmth I've never known. His

fingers trail absentmindedly along my back, tracing patterns that send shivers down my spine. I tilt my head up to meet his gaze, and his soft smile steals what little breath I have left.

"I could get used to this," I say, my voice quiet but full of emotion.

His lips twitch into a teasing grin. "I'm here at your beck and call," he replies, but there's a note of seriousness in his tone that makes my chest tighten.

I rest my hand on his chest, feeling the steady thrum of his heartbeat beneath my palm. "Good," I whisper. "Because I don't want this to end."

He cups my face, his thumb brushing gently across my cheek. "It doesn't have to," he says, his voice steady and sure. "Not if we don't want it to."

A contented sigh escapes me as I close my eyes, letting myself sink into the safety of his arms. For the first time in what feels like forever, I'm exactly where I'm meant to be. And as the world fades around us, I know that this—Cian, this moment, this love—is my happily ever after.

I hope you enjoyed *Mafia Wars*
Mafia Prince is the next book in the Young Irish Rebel Series.
Read Jack and Maeve's story.
You can download by scanning the QR code below:

Or read on for a sneak peek:

CHAPTER ONE

O'REAGAN
AN CHLANN

Maeve

The keys rattle in the door, and I press my foot to the base of the wood that normally gets jammed. Years of forcing the door open this way have damaged the base further; any day it could cave in. Pushing the door open, I hold my breath. I know the drill by now. Being away at college all week leaves my mother and brother alone, and they can barely keep themselves alive.

"Mom," I call as I force the door closed behind me. It takes three attempts before the lock slides into place, sealing me into the house. I step around the pile of cardboard that's being stacked against the skirting board. The yellow floor tiles are neglected and grubby.

The moment I step into the kitchen, I drop my bag on the floor. The table is flooded with plates with food caked onto them—the type that will take an hour of steeping to remove. I lift a pile of unopened mail and drop it back down as I scan all the empty vodka and wine bottles. Walking around the table, I force the window open and let some air filter in to try and get rid of the smell.

"Mom," I call louder as I open the back door and place a chair behind it to hold it open. My heart leaps as Sandy pounces off the counter and races out the back door. I don't even look at the counters to see what the cat's been doing. Takeaway bags and opened food are stacked high. It always looks like this when I get back from college. My weekend will be cleaning, working at the local grocery store, and trying to get some homework done.

Sandy's silver bowls are empty on the floor. I don't want to stay in the kitchen any longer, but I'm not cruel either. Opening the cupboard, I take out a moldy loaf of bread and place it on the counter. Pushing aside red sauce and some jam, I stare into emptiness. I close the cupboard and move on to the next, which holds a bag of sugar and some salt.

Sandy has re-entered the kitchen and cries up at me as she circles around my ankles.

"Yeah, I'm working on it." Kneeling down, I open the bottom cupboard and grin at the bag of cat food. Sandy leaps up on my knee, and I swipe her off.

"Here we go." I barely get the food into the bowl before Sandy's eating it. Filling up her water dish, I call my mother again before leaving the kitchen.

"Mom." She must be passed out somewhere. The sitting room door is closed, and I push it open. It takes my eyes a moment to adjust to the darkness, but once they do, I wish I could step out of the room—the air freezes in my lungs and the ground under me shifts. A man stands over my bleeding brother. My brother's gray t-shirt—that's nearly threadbare—is coated in flecks of his blood. His jeans hang off his thin frame. My gaze bounces around the scarcely furnished sitting room before landing on my mother. The air re-enters my system, and I try to control my racing heart. My mother is in a heap in the corner. Her wild eyes won't settle on anything. Mascara runs down her worn-out face. I'm tempted to step closer to her, but a shove to my back sends a shiver up my spine. The gun is nudged into my back again until I'm standing in the center of the room.

"What have we got here?"

I spin around at the voice. It's deep and holds an edge, like a sharp knife that nicks the skin. It makes me uncomfortable and cautious. Even without the gun, this man is dangerous. His bald head seems to absorb the light. Heavy brows curtain his blue eyes that assess me. He takes a step closer. The leather coat creaks as he reaches out a tattooed hand and lifts my blonde plait before dropping it back down onto my bare shoulder. I want to yank my top up, but it's meant to hang off the shoulder, so I tighten my hands into fists.

"You're a pretty little thing." His grin is razor-sharp, and alarm bells start to ring as I take a step back.

"What do you want?" My voice sounds stronger than I actually feel.

"Leave her alone." Declan moans from the floor, and I'm relieved he's alive. His pale skin had me wonder if today was the day that I would find my brother dead. Now that I see he isn't dead, I wonder what mess he has gotten us into. I try to convey my question toward him with a stare that he meets briefly. His eyes slam closed as the man above him drives his black military-style boot into my brother's stomach. I'm moving, but a hand pulls on my arm and drags me back.

"Stay where you are, bitch."

"Just tell us what you want." I can't look away from Declan as he gasps for air. The man above him grins down with enjoyment. His gaze swings to me, and he spits on my brother like he's a dog.

"Declan here owes us twelve grand."

The earth beneath my feet shifts, and I need to sit down, but I don't move. I don't look at my brother any longer as he whimpers. I want to glance at my mother, who hasn't said a word, but she's alert and watching. I can hear her useless breaths from the corner of the room.

"And if he doesn't pay?" I ask the dreaded question.

Blue eyes roam across my chest, and he takes a step closer to me, his gaze fixes on my exposed shoulder. "I was going to send your mother to one of our brothels until the debt is cleared. But now that you are here, I think you would be a very good money-spinner." His fingers reach out and grip my chin, and I'm ready to step away from him, but I hold still, and his eyes gleam with approval that I don't want.

"I could take a test drive before we agree to anything," the guy standing over my brother sneers.

"Leave my sister alone, bro. I'll get your money." Declan tries to stand, but a large boot is pressed against his chest and pushes him back down. He holds out his thin arms, and I hate how faded he looks. He's a copy of what my brother once was.

144

"Your sister?" I take a step away from Baldy as he speaks, and his fingers fall from my face. I didn't expect him to let me go so easily.

"This is the deal I'm going to make." He places the gun in the band of his trousers, and it's like the room sighs in relief. But I'm not fooled. This man would pull it out in a second. I'm keeping an eye on his friend, who I don't doubt is packing a gun as well.

"You have twenty-four hours to get me my money. If it's not here when I return, I'm taking you." His eyes bore into mine, and he takes a step toward me. This time when his fingers tighten on my arm, there is nothing gentle about it. I'm slammed against his chest as his other hand roughly dips into my pants. Terror grips me by the throat before I snap out of it, and I'm struggling. I'm trying to push him away as a deep-rooted fear starts to freeze me from the tips of my toes and travels quickly up my body. I don't want to freeze, I can't, or he will rape me. His fingers invade inside me, and then I'm free as he steps away and places his fingers in his mouth. Horror ripples through me, and my stomach lurches; It's over in a second.

"I'm nearly hoping you don't have the money. See you in twenty-four hours." His laughter floats out the door as his friend takes his foot off my brother's chest and follows him out. The moment they leave, my mother's cries grow by the second. I want to comfort her, but I'm on my knees, trying not to think about the invasion on my body.

"Declan." I'm searching his face. His soft brown eyes—the same as mine—smile up at me.

"Hi, Kiddo." His grin has always been a comfort when shit hit the fan, but now that I'm older and have taken a pounding from life, his grin doesn't comfort me; it just makes me sad, and it makes me remember what once was.

"Twelve thousand, Declan?" I shake my head, and he lies fully back. His top rises, and I hate how prominent his bones are.

"When did you last eat?" I take his arm in my hand, and he doesn't stop me as I turn it over. I expect the fresh needle marks, yet seeing them still dries up any hope that was about to flourish. Each week he makes me the same promise that he will get clean, and when I get back, he'll be a new man. The stupid part of me wants to dream that he will. I snort at my naive thoughts. Yeah, and maybe my mother will stop drinking, and my father will walk through the door. Why not go wild and let me quit my job that keeps the roof over our heads and food on the table.

"I'll get the money." Declan's smiling up at me through cracked lips that plead for water, that he doesn't even know his body is craving. I rise, and my mother continues to wail in the corner. She's managed to get her cigarettes and lighter out of her pink dressing gown pocket, so she's not that traumatized. I enter the kitchen, and the smell has me swallowing saliva. Taking down a mug, I fill it with water and return to the sitting room.

My brother drinks and slowly sits up.

"You remember that Christmas…" he's laughing at the memory that hasn't left his lips yet.

I examine his face; a cut above his eye is still bleeding.

"The one where Mum knocked over the Christmas tree, or the one where she fell into the bath?" The list was endless, but none of them were funny. Not when you craved your father to walk through the door every Christmas, but he never did. Each year I grow harder until it doesn't matter. Nothing matters, only surviving.

"The one where you swore you saw Santa Claus." Declan finally says, and his long arm wraps around his waist like he can keep the laughter in that spills from his lips and fills the room. His laughter fills the room with a small amount of light that I bask in for just a moment. I'm smiling down at my brother. It reminds me of us under his blanket late at night after our mother had passed out from drinking. Declan had a way with words, a real natural storyteller. He would take me away from our home and bring me to the magical lands of Ireland where pots of gold sat at the end of rainbows, and banshees wailed about death. He made me believe for those brief moments that maybe there was something more to this existence than this.

"It was one of Mum's boyfriends." He's still laughing, but his words sober me up.

The endless stream of men through the door never got old. Each one is as much of a write-off as my mother, who still wails in the corner like a fucking banshee from one of Declan's stories.

I'm tempted to tell her to knock it off, but I don't waste my breath. I need to bandage Declan up.

"Can you stand?"

I hate how easily I lift Declan from the floor. It's like a light sack of tinder for the fire.

"Don't leave me." My mother whimpers from the corner. Anger bubbles in my veins, and if it could morph into something more, it would scorch her.

I leave with Declan. His room is a bare mess. His bed frame is long gone. The dirty mattress on the floor is covered by a sheet that I can not lie him on. He hobbles over, and I stop him.

"I need to change it, Declan. It has sick on it."

"It's my sick."

He's ready to lie down when I whip the sheet from under him. I don't meet my brother's eyes.

"How are you going to get the money?" I ask the stupid question as I throw the sheet onto the pile of clothes next to his chest of drawers.

He lies down and groans as I pull open his curtains and let some light flitter into his room.

"Come on, Maeve, close them." He slings an arm across his eyes. But I don't close the curtains. I force open a window to let in some air.

"Declan, this is serious," I say while staring out onto our lawn that died a long time ago. My gaze travels further as a group of young people huddles together while one jams to a beat that another makes.

"I don't know how I'll get the money."

I step away from the window at my brother's admission and leave him as I grab the first aid kit in the bathroom. My mother's cries have ceased as I re-enter my brother's room and kneel down on the floor beside his mattress.

"What about Lenny?" I ask and cringe. I hate even mentioning Lenny's name. But he is a local loan shark.

My brother turns his face toward me, and I hate the sadness I see in his eyes. It's like all his pain is swimming in circles and

148

sucking the soul out of him. A force that I can't stop. My hand touches his dark hair, and I want to plead for my brother to come back to me and help me.

The weak thought has me focusing on his cut.

"Lenny broke my legs the last time," Declan says and hisses as I press down heavily on his cut.

"Yeah, well, I don't want to be raped over and over again." My words are harsh, and Declan's lanky frame goes rigid. He's five years older than me, twenty-nine, but most days, he reminds me of my little brother.

"I'll figure something out." He turns away from me onto his side. I sit with the bloodied cloth in my hand until his breathing evens out, and I know he's asleep. When he wakes, he might not even remember the threat that hangs over our heads. The bang from the hall has me freezing beside my brother. They changed their minds.

CHAPTER TWO

O'REAGAN
AN CHLANN

Jack

T he jeep sways as I cross the large steel bars that are laid at the entrance to the farmhouse. Rolling down the window, my lungs burn from the cold wind that whips its way inside the vehicle. The air pricks my skin and wakes me up a bit. How many hours had it been since I slept? Thirty-six? I had no idea. I had honestly lost count. I drive up to the red barriers that stop me from going any further. Knocking off the ignition, I reach into the back of the jeep and search for my coat. My hand skims across cold leather; I must have left my jacket in the club. Pulling the keys out, I get out reluctantly. The smell of steel and cut grass circles me as I stuff my hands into my jeans pockets and bend so I can get under the red barrier. The old farmhouse is derelict; the windows are boarded up. More grass grows on the roof than in the small patch of dirt that would be considered the front lawn.

Walking along the side of the house, I make my way to a large shed that must have housed a hundred cattle at one time. It's empty. The livestock is outside on the green patches of grass in the distance—my breath dances in front of me as I spin around at the purr of an approaching vehicle.

The job I am doing today has nothing to do with my own work; this is for my father. I stay within the clubs, running them, and maintaining order. Other parts of our operations are run by one of my uncles; they all have their roles to play. But this job today is the start of my trials. I have to prove my worth before my father passes me the crown. A white jeep pulls up behind mine. I can't see the driver, but I know who it is.

Finn, my uncle, gets out, and I curse my fucking father. Finn is nice. He never says a bad word about anyone and is known as the peacekeeper. I wanted to work with my Uncle Shane or even my Uncle Darragh. They all had their hands in the jar that my father held the lid over, ready to close it when he saw fit.

Finn waves at me, his eyes crinkle at the corners. He opens the back door and pulls out a heavy gray jacket that he slings across his body. At least he had the common sense to bring a jacket. But I couldn't see Finn any other way, only sensible and prepared.

"Finn." I greet him with a jerk of my chin as he gets closer.

"It's a cold one." He pulls a pair of gloves out of his pocket and stuffs his hands inside them.

"Mighty cold. So, what's the job?" I hope he knows more than I do, but already the fact my father sent Finn, I'm assuming this is a simple pick up. He wouldn't send Finn to harm anyone. My uncle would release them or try to talk the rest of us out of hurting anyone.

He looks so much like my Uncle Darragh. They are twins, but they are both at the opposite ends of the spectrum. Darragh's a mad bastard, always was, as far as the stories go, that I've heard countless times about him.

Finn is always wrapped in a never-ending circle of pain. They say it's from losing his wife. I don't understand his pain. I honestly think if he got laid more, he'd be better off. Of course, I'm wise enough not to voice this; no matter what I think, I have to give my respect to my elders.

"I have no idea what he sent us here for." Finn glances around the farmyard while zipping up his coat.

I pull my hands out of my jeans, and the material burns my skin. Blowing into them does little to fight off the biting cold.

Finn shrugs snugly in his jacket, and I follow him into the shed. He leans over each small wall and checks out the stalls before moving to the next.

"So, have you spoken to Cian?"

I move to the opposite side of the shed and start looking into the stalls to speed up the process. I am freezing my balls off here. "No." I keep it short, but I'm also very aware of my tone.

Finn isn't moving anymore, and I tuck my fingers under my armpits to keep them warm before turning to him.

"He's …" I'm trying to think of the right words. I want to say a complete jackass, but once again, I know I need to be careful with my words.

"I know he isn't easy."

I can't stop the sneer that tugs at my lips. "He's a red-headed little fucker." Fuck it. I've said it now.

Finn tries to hide a grin by looking over the next wall. "Don't let Shane hear you say that."

"I'm not stupid," I mumble.

"I know. That's why you will lead us." Finn's confidence in me makes me uncomfortable. I've known all my life that I would lead as the head of our family. We control all the North-East of

153

Ireland. Every drug trade, every brothel, every delivery of arms, we controlled. My dad and his brothers had built it up from nothing, and the empire that sat before me had hotels, clubs, restaurants, and an endless portfolio of property. I should be ecstatic to be inheriting everything, but it isn't that simple. Nothing good ever is.

"Found it." Finn's words drag me out of my thoughts, and I bounce across the shed towards him. He steps into the last stall. Of course, it's at the end, the furthest distance away from the jeeps. I pull back the green tarp, and I stare at the white blocks that are stacked nearly five feet high.

"That's a lot of coke. Are we expected to load this into the Jeeps?"

"No. We just stare at it and then leave it here." Finn's sarcasm is unexpected, and when he glances at me, I can see he's ready to apologize. I don't want his apology.

I grab two blocks of white powder and turn to Finn. He still wears a grin—the air ripples before warm liquid splatters across my face. Finn hits the ground, and I'm standing frozen as I blink several times. The gurgling at my feet has me dropping the white blocks, and I join Finn on the ground.

He's trying to breathe, but he reminds me of a fish out of water, gasping for air. Blood pours from his neck. His hands grip the wound, but blood oozes out far too quickly. I'm waiting for more bullets to rain down on us, but the air is still. The shooter has ceased or has left. I want to find him and make him pay for spilling O'Reagan blood. Already I'm fueled with thoughts of revenge.

Finn's blue eyes are fading, and there is a wild panic in them that I've seen before, in dying animals and people.

"You're not dying today." I push a hand down over the wound while getting out my phone.

My father doesn't answer, and I curse him before I ring Shane.

"Finn's been shot." I want to add, 'and it's bad.'

"I'm on the way." Shane hangs up and doesn't ask where we are. They would all know since this was part of the trials. I rub my face into my shoulder to try to get rid of the blood that still coats my face.

My hand turns red, and Finn's skin pales even further. All I can think of is that he can't die on my watch. This wasn't part of the trials. The blood that runs from him is warm; this isn't a trick or a test. Someone just shot my uncle. Maybe he wasn't the target. Maybe I was. I raise my head slightly but can't see much over the wall.

"Shane is on his way," I speak to Finn, and his eyes flutter closed.

"Stay awake, Finn."

His eyes open, but he isn't with me at this moment. He's somewhere else.

"Don't you fucking stop fighting," I warn and press my hand down heavier on his neck. All I can do is talk shit to him, to keep him awake. I'm telling him anything I can think of. I'm ten again.

"I met your dad once. My grandfather."

I swear it looks like his eyes widen.

"He said he just wanted to meet me, get to know me. He looks like you all." I listen for the purr of a vehicle that I don't hear.

Where are you, Shane?

"He said I was part of An Chlann."

Finn gargles as he tries to speak.

"Shut the fuck up, Finn." Panic tears through me. I don't want to hear his dying words. I won't be the one to watch the light go out in his eyes. A car tears into the yard.

"See, everything is going to be fine. Shane's here."

Hope doesn't blossom in Finn's eyes.

A car door shuts.

"The last stall," I shout. Once again, I'm tempted to say how bad it is, but I don't. "The shot came from the west. The shooter could still be here."

"Is it bad?" Shane's voice is closer.

I want to growl and tell him to hurry up.

"It's a neck shot."

Shane curses, and he appears. He stares at his brother on the ground.

"Finn." He kneels down, and his eyes roam across Finn's face and neck.

Finn's still alert, and I don't know how. *You can't kill a bad thing*; that's what my father always said. Only Finn isn't a bad person. He was the only good in all of us.

"We lift him on the count of three."

I'm gripping his legs, and Shane takes his shoulders. I hate as we rise how blood puddles on the ground. We leave a trail through the shed and all the way to the car.

Once he's loaded into the back of Shane's car, I'm ready to climb in.

"Stay here. Darragh will be arriving to help you clean up."

"What about Finn?" I can't see him now because Shane has laid him flat in the backseat.

Shane pulls the door closed and reverses like the Gardaí are chasing him. I don't move from the spot for a moment until my phone starts to ring.

"Shane arrived. He's taking Finn to the hospital."

"Darragh and Cian are on their way," My father says. I didn't want to have to look at Cian, but right now wasn't the time to start mouthing off. I climb into the Jeep, leaving bloodied handprints everywhere.

Any brother would ask how his brother is after he's been shot, but not my father.

"Did you get a look at the shooter?" His line of questioning is so typical of him. Find the threat and eliminate it. The rest is collateral damage. I wonder if it were me flapping around like a fucking fish on the ground, he would still react the same.

"No," I answer.

"Did you look around?"

I grit my teeth and stare down at my hands. "No, Shane just left."

"The moment Darragh and Cian arrive, scout the area. Find something, Jack."

"I will."

I glance in the rear-view mirror as Darragh's BMW pulls up. The red-headed fucker is so tall in the front that he's hunched over.

"Darragh is here."

"Okay, ring me if you find anything." My father's voice is so formal.

I'm ready to hang up when he pauses, making me pause.

"Son, be careful."

Dread tightens around the base of my spine; my father never said anything like that before. I want to question him, but he hangs up. Darragh's at my window lighting a cigarette

I get out, and he moves back.

His eyes dance to my hands, and I see real fear in Darragh's eyes.

"He's gone to the hospital with Shane."

Cian steps around Darragh. He's nearly seven-foot-tall and

towers over us all. He wears his normal snarl as he places a huge hand on Darragh's shoulder.

"He's in good hands."

I scratch the back of my neck and stop when wet liquid touches the sensitive skin.

"What can you tell us?" Cian's wearing a gray jacket with the collar standing up like some fucking golfer. He's a right prick.

His words irritate me. "Nothing." I start to walk before I punch him in the throat. Instead of focusing on him, I draw all my attention to Darragh, who chain smokes.

"One single shot was fired from the west. So I'm going to scout the area."

"Where was he shot?"

"The neck." I jerk my chin toward the last stall.

Darragh curses as he glances down at the trail of blood that leads to the last stall.

"I'll scout the area with Jack." Cian offers up, and I'm already walking away, hoping he'll pick up on my subtle way of saying fuck off. If he had been shot and was gargling on the ground, I think I would have stood on his neck.

"So, you saw nothing?"

I clench my jaw. "No."

A high bank rises, and I start to climb. Cian is right behind me. Once I reach the top, I look for tracks, something that will tell me where the shooter was. I keep walking and look up. I'm close to the shed, but he would have had to have been further down to take the shot. Cian pulls out a gun and moves in front of me. I don't stop him. If he wants to be a shield, by all means, be a fucking shield.

"You think he's still here?" He asks.

How was he so tall? Shane was over six feet, but his mother, Una, was five feet. He got her red hair.

"If he is, he would have shot us by now." The logical part of my brain tells me, but I'm still fine with Cian going first.

He stops at a spot, and I walk around him. The grass here has been flattened. I lie in the exact same spot and can see the last stall where Finn and I had stood. He could have shot either of us. He chose to shoot Finn. My fingers trace the grass, searching for anything, but there is nothing left. The area is cold. "He's gone."

My phone rings in my pocket, and I stand up and pull it out.

"It's really bad." Shane's words have me lowering myself to the ground as I wait for the final blow, as I wait for him to tell me that Finn is dead.

Download and read:

Other Books by VI Carter

THE O'SULLIVAN'S BRIDES

When Kings Rise #1

When Kings Bend#2

When Kings Fall#3

THE CELLS OF KALASHOV

The Collector #1

The Handler #2

The Sixth #3

SONS OF THE MAFIA

Vengeance in Blood #1

Enemies in Ruin #2

Redemption in Cruelty #3

Mercy in Betrayal #4

Vows in Violence #5

STANDALONES

Dark Desires

SHORT STORIES

Bought by the Billionaire

Thorn

ABOUT THE AUTHOR

Vi Carter - the queen of *DARK ROMANCE*, the mistress of suspense, and the high priestess of *PLOT TWISTS*!

When she's not busy crafting tales of the *MAFIA* that'll leave you on the edge of your seat, you can find her baking up a storm, exploring the gorgeous Irish countryside, or spending time with her three little girls.

Vi's Young Irish Rebels series has been praised by readers and can be found in English, Dutch, German, Audible and soon will be available in French.

And let's not forget her two greatest loves: *coffee and chocolate*. If you ever need to bribe her, just offer up a mug of coffee and a slab of chocolate, and she'll be putty in your hands.

So, if you're ready to join Vi on a wild journey with the mafia, sign up for her newsletter and score a free book! Just be warned - her stories are so *ADDICTIVE*, you might not be able to put them down.

WHAT READERS ARE SAYING

EDITORIAL REVIEWS

"Vi Carter has once again blown my mind with another outstanding story. She never fails to create a masterpiece with memorable characters that leap off the page. This book is complete perfection."- USA Today Bestselling Author Khardine Gray

Vi is one of those authors who never disappoints. She weaves *LOVE & DANGER* effortlessly. ★★★★★ stars

I definitely recommend this book. It is *SUSPENSEFUL* and exciting. I enjoy reading Vi Carter's book. ★★★★★ stars

HOW TO KEEP IN TOUCH WITH VI CARTER

Visit Vi's website: https://author-vicarter.com/.

Join the newsletter: t.ly/yZWbX

Or scan the code below:

On Facebook, Instagram, TikTok and YouTube @ darkauthorvicarter and on Twitter @authorvicarter

Or scan the code below:

ACKNOWLEDGMENTS

I'm very lucky to have such amazing readers and Beta Readers. I want to thank the following Beta Readers who worked with me on this book.

Beta Readers
Tami Thomason
Lucy Korth

Proofreader
Sherry Schafer

Cover Designer
Elise Hoffman

Formatter
Elise Hoffman

Mafia Wars